A

Vivienne was totally rattled; this was the second time that day that Jack had somehow turned her on. Not consciously, of course. Or deliberately. He would have no idea what mad thoughts he'd been evoking.

She pulled her eyes away, then did what she always did when life threatened to overwhelm her. She concentrated on the matter at hand.

'So, Jack,' she said, looking back at him with her business face on, 'tell me exactly what the terms of my employment will be.'

Jack frowned. 'If you come with me tomorrow you can inspect Francesco's Folly for yourself and tell me how long you think the job will take to complete. At the same time, given that you would be doing me a special favour by taking this job, I am prepared to be generous.'

Vivienne's eyebrows lifted. Jack Stone was not known for his generosity. He was a fair businessman, but tough.

'*How* generous?' she asked.

'*Very* generous.'

'But why? I'm sure you could get any number of up-and-coming young designers to do the job for next to nothing.'

'I don't want any other up-and-coming designer, Vivienne. I want *you*.'

Miranda Lee is Australian, and lives near Sydney. Born and raised in the bush, she was boarding-school-educated, and briefly pursued a career in classical music before moving to Sydney and embracing the world of computers. Happily married, with three daughters, she began writing when family commitments kept her at home. She likes to create stories that are believable, modern, fast-paced and sexy. Her interests include meaty sagas, doing word puzzles, gambling and going to the movies.

Recent titles by the same author:

MASTER OF HER VIRTUE
CONTRACT WITH CONSEQUENCES
THE MAN EVERY WOMAN WANTS
NOT A MARRYING MAN

Did you know these are also available as eBooks?
Visit www.millsandboon.co.uk

A MAN
WITHOUT MERCY

BY
MIRANDA LEE

MILLS & BOON

Published in Great Britain 2014
by Mills & Boon, an imprint of Harlequin (UK) Limited,
Eton House, 18-24 Paradise Road, Richmond, Surrey, TW9 1SR

© 2014 Miranda Lee

ISBN: 978 0 263 24144 0

Harlequin (UK) Limited's policy is to use papers that are natural, renewable and recyclable products and made from wood grown in sustainable forests. The logging and manufacturing processes conform to the legal environmental regulations of the country of origin.

Printed and bound in Great Britain
by CPI Antony Rowe, Chippenham, Wiltshire

A MAN
WITHOUT MERCY

CHAPTER ONE

'WHAT DO YOU mean, I *can't* have Vivienne?' Jack said. 'I *always* have Vivienne.'

Nigel suppressed a sigh. He didn't like disappointing his best client but there was nothing he could do about it.

'Sorry, Jack, but as of yesterday Miss Swan doesn't work for Classic Design any longer.'

Jack's head jerked back with shock. 'You *fired* her?'

Now it was Nigel's turn to look startled. 'Hardly. Vivienne was one of my best designers. No,' he added, with true regret in his voice. 'She quit.'

Jack could not contain his surprise at this second piece of news. Admittedly, he didn't know Vivienne all that well, despite her having worked for him on his last three building projects. She was an extremely self-contained young woman who didn't engage in idle chit-chat. When on a job, her focus was always on her work, which was simply brilliant. He had asked her not long ago why she didn't open her own interior design firm, and she'd replied that she didn't want that kind of stress, especially now that she was engaged to be married. She'd said she didn't want to live just for work any longer, a sentiment which Jack had not appreciated—till yesterday.

He'd been driving around the Port Stephens area, looking for suitable land for another retirement village, when he'd come across a small acreage for sale which had totally blown him away. It wasn't what he was looking for, not even remotely. Not the right kind of land, for starters; not flat enough. There'd also been a huge house smack dab in the middle of the lot, perched on top of a hill. A house unlike anything Jack had ever seen, with a name that was as unique as the building.

Despite knowing he was wasting his time, Jack had still felt compelled to inspect Francesco's Folly. From the moment he'd walked inside and out onto the first of the many balconies which all faced the bay, he'd known he wanted the place. Not only wanted it but wanted to live in it. Crazy, really, since Port Stephens was a good three-hour drive north of Sydney. Jack's normal place of residence was a conveniently located and relatively modest three-bedroomed apartment in the same CBD building which housed his construction company's head office. Aside from its inconvenient location, Francesco's Folly was as far removed from modest as a residence could get, with eight bedrooms, six bathrooms and an indoor/outdoor swimming pool which would have put a Hollywood mansion to shame.

As a confirmed bachelor who never entertained at home, Jack had no need for a house this size, but it was no use. He simply had to have it, telling himself that maybe it was time for him to relax and live a little. After all, he'd been flogging himself for two decades, working six and sometimes seven days a week, making millions in the process. Why shouldn't he indulge himself for once? He didn't actually have to live in the place twenty-four-seven. He could use it as a weekender, or a holiday home. So could the rest of his family. Thinking of their pleasure at having such a dream place at their disposal had sealed the deal for Jack, so he'd bought Francesco's Folly that very afternoon, getting it for a bargain, partly because it was a deceased estate, but mostly because the interior was hideously dated—hence his need for an excellent interior designer, one whose taste and work ethics matched his. It annoyed Jack considerably that the one person whom he could trust to do the job, and do it well, was unavailable to him.

But then it suddenly occurred to Jack that maybe that wasn't the case.

'So who was the sneaky devil who head-hunted her?' he demanded to know, excited by the possibility that he could still hire the decorator he wanted for the job.

'Vivienne hasn't gone to work for anyone else,' Nigel informed him.

'How do you know?'

'She told me so. Look, Jack, if you must know, Vivienne's not feeling well at the moment. She's decided to have some time off work.'

Jack was taken back. 'What do you mean, not feeling well? What's the matter with her?'

'I guess it doesn't matter if I tell you. It's not as though it isn't public knowledge.'

Jack frowned. It certainly wasn't public knowledge to him.

Nigel frowned also. 'I'm guessing by the look on your face that you didn't read the gossip columns in Sunday's papers, or see the photos.'

'I never read gossip columns,' Jack replied. He did sometimes skim through the Sunday paper—mostly the property section—but he'd been busy yesterday. 'So what did I miss? Though, truly, I can't imagine a girl like Vivienne making it into any gossip column. She isn't the type.'

'It wasn't Vivienne. It was her ex-fiancé.'

'*Ex*-fiancé… Good Lord, when did that happen? She was solidly engaged last time I saw her a few weeks back.'

'Yes, well, Daryl broke off their engagement about a month ago. Told her he'd fallen in love with someone else. The poor girl was shattered, but she was very brave and soldiered on. Of course, the rat claimed he hadn't cheated on her whilst they were still engaged, but yesterday's paper proved that was just rubbish.'

'For pity's sake, Nigel, just tell me what was in the darned paper!'

'The thing is, the girl Daryl dumped Vivienne for wasn't just any old girl. He left her for Courtney Ellison. You know…? Frank Ellison's spoiled daughter. Vivienne did the decorating job on the harbourside mansion you built for Ellison, so I guess that's how the two lovebirds met. Anyway, the bit in the gossip column was announcing their engagement. In the photos—there were several—the Ellison girl is sporting a diamond engagement ring the size of an egg—as well as a much bigger baby-bump, meaning their affair's been going on for quite some time.

'Naturally, there was no mention of Courtney's handsome husband-to-be having been recently engaged to another woman. Darling Daddy would have quashed that. You don't get to be a billionaire mining magnate in this country without having lots of connections in the media. As you can imagine, Vivienne is very cut up about it. She was in tears on the phone yesterday, which is not like her at all.'

Jack could not have agreed more. Tears were not

Vivienne's style. He'd never met any female as cool and collected as Vivienne. But he supposed everyone had their breaking point. He shook his head, regretting now that he'd recommended her to Frank Ellison. Jack hated to think that he was in some way responsible for Vivienne's unhappiness. But how could he possibly have known that Ellison's man-eating maniac of a daughter would get her claws into Vivienne's fiancé?

Still…if ever there was a man willing and ready to be eaten by the likes of Courtney Ellison, it was Vivienne's now ex-fiancé.

Jack had only met Daryl once—when he'd briefly dropped in on Classic Design's Christmas party last year—but once had been enough to form an opinion. Okay, so darling Daryl was movie-star good-looking. And charming, he supposed, if you liked silver-tongued talkers who smiled a lot, touched a lot and called their fiancée 'babe'. Clearly, Vivienne did, since she'd been planning on marrying him.

It saddened Jack that Vivienne had been unlucky enough to lose her heart to one of that ilk, but he had no doubt that she would, in time, see that she'd had a narrow escape from long-term misery as a result of Daryl's defection. Meanwhile, the last thing that girl needed was to be allowed to wallow in her present misery. Jack understood that Vivienne was probably feeling wretched, but nothing would be achieved by cutting herself off from the one thing she was good at and would make her feel good about herself: her work.

'I see,' he said, quickly deciding on a course of action. 'You wouldn't have Vivienne's address, would you, Nigel? I'd like to send her some flowers,' he added before Nigel gave him some bulldust about privacy issues.

Nigel stared at Jack for a long moment before looking up the company files on his computer and writing down the address.

'I don't like your chances,' he said as he handed the address over.

'My chances of what?' Jack replied, poker-faced.

Nigel smiled a dry smile. 'Come now, Jack, you and I both know you don't want Vivienne's address just to send her flowers. You're going to hotfoot it over to her place and try to get her to do whatever it is you want her to do. Which is what, by the way? Another retirement-home project?'

'No,' Jack said, despite thinking that Francesco's Folly would make a perfect retirement home, when and if he ever actually retired. 'It's a personal project, a holiday house I've bought which badly needs redecorating. Look, it'll do Vivienne good to keep busy.'

'She's very fragile at the moment,' Nigel warned. 'Not everyone is as tough as you, Jack.'

'I've often found that the gentler sex are a lot tougher than we men think they are,' Jack said as he stood up and extended his hand in parting.

Nigel tried not to wince when Jack's large hand closed around his much smaller one. But truly, the man didn't know his own strength sometimes. Didn't know women as well as he thought he did, either. No way was Vivienne going to let herself be bulldozed into working for him. Aside from the fact that she was in a dreadful emotional state at the moment, she'd never overly liked the owner of Stone Constructions—something which Jack obviously didn't know.

But privately she'd expressed the opinion to Nigel that Jack was a pain in the neck to work for, a driven workaholic with impossibly high standards which, whilst admirable in one way, could be very trying. Of course, he did pay very well, but that wasn't going to help him where Vivienne was concerned. Money had never interested her all that much, possibly because she'd inherited plenty of her own when her mother had died a couple of years ago.

'If you want some advice,' Nigel called after Jack as he headed for the door, 'Actually taking Vivienne some flowers—not red roses, mind you—might improve your chances of success.'

Though Nigel seriously doubted it.

CHAPTER TWO

VIVIENNE'S ADDRESS WAS easy to find. It was located in Neutral Bay, only a short drive from Classic Design's office in North Sydney. Finding a florist first was not quite so easy. Neither was deciding what flowers to buy. By the time Jack parked outside the two-storey red-brick building which housed Vivienne's apartment, an hour had passed since he'd left Nigel.

Not a man who liked wasting time, it was a some-what exasperated Jack who climbed out from behind the wheel of his black Porsche, carrying the basket of pink and white carnations the florist had finally convinced him to buy.

A sudden autumn shower had Jack bolting up the narrow front path and into the small lobby of the apartment block. Thankfully, he didn't get too wet, just a few drops on his shoulders and hair; nothing that couldn't be easily remedied.

There wasn't any security panel anywhere, he noted as he smoothed back his hair. The building was quite old, possibly federation, though in reasonably good condition. He pressed the brass door-bell, hearing only a faint ring coming from inside. No one came to answer straight away, giving rise to the annoying possibility that Vivienne wasn't at home. Jack now regretted not ringing first. He had her mobile number in his phone. He'd just presumed she'd be at home after what Nigel had said.

'I'm a bloody idiot,' he muttered under his breath as he pulled his phone out of his pocket and brought Vivienne's number up on the menu. He was about to call when he heard the dead lock being turned. It wasn't Vivienne who opened the door, however, but a plump, middle-aged woman with short blonde hair and a kind face.

'Yes?' she said. 'Can I help you?'

'I hope so,' Jack replied, switching off his phone and slipping it back into his jeans pocket. 'Is Vivienne at home?'

'Well, yes, but…um…she's taking a bath at the moment. I presume those flowers are for her? If you give them to me, I'll make sure she gets them.'

'I'd prefer to give them to her personally, if you don't mind.'

The woman frowned at him. 'And who might you be?'

'The name's Jack. Jack Stone. Vivienne's worked for me on a number of occasions.'

'Ah yes. Mr Stone. Vivienne has mentioned you once or twice.'

Jack was taken aback by the dry tone in the woman's voice when she said that. He wondered momentarily what Vivienne had said about him, but then dismissed the thought as irrelevant.

'And you are?' he shot back.

'Marion Havers. I live in number two,' she said, nodding towards the adjoining door. 'Vivienne and I are good friends as well as neighbours. Look, I presume since you've brought her flowers that you know what's happened.'

'Actually, I didn't know a thing till I went to Classic Design's office this morning to hire Vivienne for a job. Nigel explained the situation, saying how upset Vivienne was, so I thought I'd come round and see how she was.'

'How very kind of you,' the woman said with a soft sigh. 'As you can imagine, the poor girl's devastated. Can't eat. Can't sleep. She did get some sleeping tablets from the doctor, but they don't seem to be working too well. Anyway, after this latest catastrophe, I think she'll be needing some serious anti-depressants.'

Jack had never agreed with the way people turned to medication to solve life's problems.

'What Vivienne needs, Marion,' he said sternly, 'is to keep busy. Which is the main reason I'm here: I was hoping to persuade her to come and work for me.'

Marion looked at him as though he were delusional, but then she shrugged. 'You can try, I suppose. But I don't like your chances.'

Frankly, he thought he stood a darned good chance. Okay, so Vivienne was very upset at the moment, but beneath her distress she was still the same sensible young woman he'd come to respect enormously. She'd soon see the logic in his proposal.

'Could I come inside,' Jack asked, 'and wait till Vivienne's finished in the bathroom? I really would appreciate a personal word with her today.'

Marion looked doubtful for a moment, until she glanced at her wristwatch. 'I suppose it will be all right. I don't have to leave for work for another half hour. Vivienne should be out of the bath by then.' She looked up at him and smiled. 'Meanwhile, I could do with a quick cuppa. Would you like to join me? Or would you prefer coffee?'

Jack smiled back at her. 'Tea will be fine.'

'Good. Here, give me those flowers and follow me. And close the door after you,' she threw over her shoulder.

Marion led him down a narrow hallway which had a very high ceiling, white walls and polished floorboards the colour of walnut. Jack passed three shut doors on his left before the hallway opened into a living room which surprised him by being so starkly furnished. It didn't look anything like the stylish but comfy living rooms Vivienne decorated for him in his show homes.

Jack glanced around with disbelieving eyes. Where were the warm feminine touches which were her trademark? There were no colourful cushions or elegant lamps; no display cabinets or shelves; no ornaments of any kind, not even a photo on display. Just one long black leather sofa with a neutral-shaded shag rug in front of it and a chunky wooden coffee-table varnished the same colour as the floors.

Only one picture graced the white walls, a black-framed painting showing a girl dressed in a red coat, walking alone along a rain-spattered city street. Obviously a quality painting, but not one Jack found pleasure in looking at. Despite wearing red, the girl looked sad and cold. Like this whole room.

It occurred to Jack that possibly dear old Daryl had stripped the room of some things when he had left, which could account for its ultra-bare look. He wasn't sure how he knew Daryl had been living here with Vivienne, but he *was* sure. She must have said something at some stage. Or maybe Daryl had, at that Christmas party. Yes, that was it: he'd mentioned he was moving in with her in the New Year. Whatever; maybe there had been more furniture in this room before he'd left and more pictures on the walls, plus the odd photo or two. The TV was still there, Jack noted, mounted on the wall opposite the sofa. But one would have expected a piece of furniture underneath it—a sideboard of some kind. There was room for it.

Marion stopped briefly to deposit the basket of carnations on the coffee table before leading him on into the kitchen which, though smallish, was brilliantly designed to incorporate every mod con and still leave enough space for a table and four chairs. Obviously, it had been remodelled recently, since the bench tops *and* the table top were made in the kind of stone which had only become popular during the last few years. White, of course; white was *the* colour for kitchens these days. That and stainless-steel appliances. Vivienne always insisted on that combination in kitchens she designed for him. But she usually introduced a bit of colour in the splashbacks as well as other decorative touches: a bowl of fruit here and there. A vase of flowers. And, yes, something colourful on the walls.

There was nothing like that here in Vivienne's place, however. If it *was* hers? Jack suddenly wondered. Possibly this was a rental. He hadn't thought of that. Only one way to find out, he supposed.

'Does Vivienne own this place?' he asked as he pulled out one of the white leather-backed chairs which surrounded the table.

Marion glanced over her shoulder from where she was making the tea. 'Sure does. Bought it when she inherited some money a while back. Had it refurbished from top to bottom last year. Not quite to my taste, but we all like different things, don't we? Vivienne's one of those women who can't bear clutter.'

'I can see that,' Jack remarked.

'Would you like a biscuit or two with your tea?' Marion asked.

'Please,' Jack replied. It was nearly one o'clock and he hadn't eaten since breakfast.

'How do you have your tea?'

'Black, with no sugar.'

Marion sighed a somewhat exasperated sigh as she carried Jack's mug of tea, plus a plate of cream biscuits, over to the table. 'Lord knows what Vivienne's doing in that bathroom. She's been in there for ages.'

Their eyes met, Jack's chest tightening when sudden alarm filled Marion's face.

'Perhaps you should knock on the door and let her know I'm here,' he suggested.

'Yes. Yes, I think I'll do that,' Marion said, and hurried off.

Jack listened to her footsteps on the polished floorboards, then to her knocking on a door, along with her anxious-sounding voice. 'Vivienne, are you nearly finished in there? I have to go to work soon and you have a visitor—Jack Stone. He wants to speak to you. Vivienne, can you hear me?'

When Jack heard even louder knocking and obviously still no answer from Vivienne, he jumped to his feet and raced down to where Marion was standing at the first door past the living room.

'She won't answer me, Jack,' the woman said frantically. 'And the door's locked. You don't think she's done anything silly, do you?'

Jack wasn't sure of anything, so he banged on the door himself.

'Vivienne,' he called out loudly at the same time.
'It's Jack. Jack Stone. Will you open the door, please?'

Not a word in reply.

'Bloody hell,' he muttered as he examined the bathroom door which was solid wood, as opposed to chipboard, but also ancient and hopefully the victim of termites over the years. Telling Marion to stand back, he shoulder-charged it with every ounce of strength he had, splintering the lock in the process and taking the door right off at the hinges.

Jack half-fell into the bathroom, taking a second or two to right himself and see what the situation was.

Vivienne wasn't lying comatose or drowned under the water, the victim of an overdose of sleeping tablets. She was alive and well, bolting upright in the bath as the commotion of the door being shattered finally penetrated the earplugs she'd been wearing. Her piercing scream testified to her shock, her mouth staying open as she gaped at Jack.

On his part, Jack just stood there in the mangled doorway, totally speechless. He hadn't stopped to think about Vivienne being naked. All he'd been concerned about a few seconds earlier was her safety. Now, suddenly, all he could think about *was* her nakedness. His eyes were transfixed on her bare breasts which were, without doubt, the most beautiful breasts he'd ever seen. They glistened at him, two lushly rounded globes, their smooth, pale flesh centred with dusky-pink aureoles and crowned with the most tantalisingly erect nipples.

Jack had never thought of Vivienne as busty before, perhaps because she always wore tailored suits and shirt-like blouses, which obviously covered up her curves. He recalled that, even at that Christmas party he'd attended, she'd worn a loose-fitting dress which had successfully hidden her knockout figure, one which would have any red-blooded heterosexual male salivating over her.

Unfortunately, Jack was a red-blooded heterosexual male who hadn't been with a woman since back in early March, over two months ago. Hell, had it been that long? It obviously had, by the uncomfortable stirring in his jeans.

Thank goodness Marion pushed past him at that stage and started rapidly explaining things to a still gaping Vivienne. Dragging his eyes off those stunning breasts, Jack spun round and marched back to the kitchen, telling himself ruefully as he sat down and munched into a biscuit that he really had to get himself a life. A sex life, that was. He was, after all, only thirty-seven years old, a fit, virile man still in his sexual prime. He couldn't keep restricting himself to holiday flings, or the occasional one-night stand. He needed sex on a more regular basis.

But that would mean getting himself a proper girlfriend, something Jack was reluctant to do. He'd had girlfriends before and they had always wanted more than just sex. They wanted to go on regular dates, attend family gatherings and, ultimately, they wanted a ring on their finger. Even if they were prepared to bypass marriage and just live with a guy, inevitably they still wanted children.

Jack didn't want children. For the past twenty years he'd been father as well as big brother to his two younger sisters, protecting and providing for them, along with his mother, who'd been totally useless when she'd unexpectedly become a widow at the young age of forty. Jack himself had only been seventeen when his father had been killed in a motor-cycle accident. After it was discovered that his dad had been hopeless with money, with no insurance premiums up to date and more debts than you could poke a stick at, his mother had promptly fallen to pieces, leaving it up to him to become the man of the house. Jack had been obliged to leave school immediately and get work so that they could survive.

It had nearly killed him to abandon his ambition to become an engineer, but he'd had no alternative. There was simply no one else he could turn to for financial help. Jack had worked as a builder's labourer seven days a week to cover the mortgage and put food on the table. Fortunately, he'd been a big lad who could handle the gruelling workload. Also, he'd been smart enough to learn most of the building trades in record time and eventually set up a building business of his own, one which had earned him more than enough over the years to provide for himself and his family.

Jack no longer regretted not becoming an engineer. He loved what he did. He loved his family, too; very much. But providing for and protecting them all these years had taken an emotional toll on him. There was simply no room left in his heart for another family. He didn't want a wife of his own. Or children. What he did want, however, was more sex.

But getting more sex wasn't as easy as some people seemed to think. Okay, so Jack didn't have much trouble picking up women when he put his mind to it. But at thirty-seven his appetite for one-night stands had faded somewhat. Nowadays, he preferred to have sex with a woman he actually liked, not just one he lusted after.

What he needed, he decided, was a mistress, someone attractive and intelligent he could visit on a regular basis but who wouldn't put any emotional or social demands on him.

Jack was mulling over this problem when Marion bustled into the room.

'Sorry, Jack, but I really must go get changed for work. Vivienne said for you to wait here. She won't be long. Nice to have met you,' she added before hurrying off through a back door.

Jack grimaced at the thought of being left alone with a no doubt even more upset Vivienne. Lord knew what she must have thought when he'd burst into the bathroom like that.

'I dare say she's not too happy about the bathroom door, either,' he was muttering when the woman herself swept into the kitchen wrapped in a fluffy white robe and matching slippers.

'You can say that again,' Vivienne snapped as she tightened the sash around her waist.

The thought that she was still naked underneath her dressing gown was decidedly unsettling. So was the fact that her hair was down, long auburn waves falling in disarray around her shoulders. Jack had never seen her with her hair down before. Had no idea it was that long. Or that pretty. It was usually pulled back off her face into some kind of roll thing which was both practical and professional-looking. He was sure she hadn't worn it down at the Christmas party he'd attended, either. He would have noticed.

Or would he?

Jack never paid too much personal attention to females he worked with, or who belonged to another man. He'd learned over the years not to complicate his life by inviting trouble with members of the opposite sex. Yes, he'd been aware that Vivienne was an attractive girl, but that was as far as his observations had gone.

Now, as his eyes lifted to study her face more closely,

he discovered that she was more than attractive. She was really quite beautiful, with delicate bone structure, a small, straight nose, full lips and the most gorgeous green eyes. How in hell he hadn't noticed those eyes, he had no idea. Perhaps because she wore sunglasses most of the time.

He sure as hell noticed them now, since they were glaring at him with the kind of fury that might have made a lesser man quiver in his boots.

'I expect you to have that door fixed as soon as possible,' Vivienne demanded.

'I'll get right on to it today,' he agreed.

'I can't imagine why you thought I was actually in there topping myself,' she went on heatedly. 'The very idea is ludicrous!'

Jack wished he'd trusted his instinct that Vivienne wasn't the suicidal type. But it was too late now.

'Marion said you'd been in there a very long time,' he explained, hoping his calm tone would soothe her temper. 'And then, of course, there was what Nigel told me earlier this morning.'

'Oh yes?' she said, crossing her arms and giving him a very droll look. 'And just what did Nigel say about me?'

Jack decided sarcasm was a definite improvement on white-hot rage. 'He said that I couldn't hire you for a job because you'd quit.'

'Hmph!' Vivienne snorted. 'I'll bet that's not all he said.'

'No. He told me what had happened with Daryl and the Ellison girl.'

'Indeed,' Vivienne said, her chin suddenly beginning to quiver as it did when a girl was about to cry.

Jack was very familiar with the symptom. He held

his breath, not sure what he would do if she started weeping. He didn't like the thought of having to comfort her physically. Hugging crying sisters and mothers was rather different from hugging a woman he was finding terribly sexy all of a sudden. And there was something provocative about Vivienne spitting fire at him just now. He had an awful feeling that if he took her in his arms at this moment he might do something really stupid. Like kiss her. Which would put a swift end to his plan to get her to redecorate Francesco's Folly. Vivienne would no doubt slap his face then tell him in no uncertain terms to get lost. As it was, Jack knew he would still have the devil of a time persuading her to take the job.

Luckily, she didn't dissolve into tears, her jaw firming and her eyes flashing with a defiant glitter.

'Well, that was yesterday!' she stated with the kind of spirit Jack could not help but admire. 'Today is another day. So, Jack,' she went on, sitting down in the chair opposite him, 'what is this job you wanted to hire me for?'

CHAPTER THREE

VIVIENNE FOUND THE surprised expression on Jack Stone's normally stone-like face somewhat satisfying. So, he was not a machine after all! Okay, so he *had* stared at her breasts in the bathroom just now. But not the way most men would have stared. There'd been no lust in his piercing blue eyes. There'd been nothing but shock. Possibly because she wasn't dead, as he'd imagined.

It had shaken Vivienne when Marion had explained that was what they'd both been thinking, making her see how her very uncharacteristic behaviour—especially her rather hysterical quitting of her job—would worry the people who truly cared about her. Not Jack, of course. Vivienne wasn't silly enough to think Jack Stone cared about her. She knew him better than that. His showing up here and bringing her flowers was just a ploy to get her to do what he wanted. He didn't give a damn if her heart was broken, as long as she agreed to what he had in mind work-wise.

And her heart *was* broken.

It was bad enough to be told that the man she loved no longer loved her. Worse was finally finding out who it was he'd left her for. Even worse was seeing the size of Courtney Ellison's baby bump.

The realisation that Daryl had been cheating on her for months had been devastating. Mostly because she'd believed him when he'd insisted he hadn't slept with his new love as yet.

God, she couldn't bear to think about how stupid and gullible she'd been where that man was concerned.

She would *not* think about it any more, she vowed staunchly. Instead, she steeled her spine and eyed Jack with what she hoped was a steadfast gaze. The last thing she wanted to do was break down in front of the likes of him.

'Well?' she said sharply. 'Out with it.'

His blue eyes darkened, his thick dark brows bunching together in a puzzled frown.

Another first, Vivienne thought with perverse triumph. First surprise and now confusion.

'Are you saying you'll actually consider my proposal?' he asked.

Vivienne laughed. 'Not if it's a proposal of marriage. But I'm prepared to consider a work proposal. It's occurred to me that I was foolish to quit my job, especially if it's going to make people think I'm about to top myself. So yes, Jack, tell me what you want me to do, and if I like the idea I'll do it.'

Once again, Jack gave her a look unlike any he'd ever given her. He also did something else: he smiled, a slow almost amused smile which was annoyingly unreadable.

Vivienne wondered what she'd said that had tickled his fancy. Possibly her crack about a marriage proposal. It was well known around the building world that Jack Stone was a confirmed bachelor. No surprise there. How could he be anything else? The man was a workaholic. He wouldn't have time for a wife and a family. She'd never seen him with a girlfriend in tow, either. Not on site at any of his building projects, or even at last year's Christmas party.

Vivienne suspected, however, that he didn't live the life of a monk. He was too male for that. 'Testosterone on legs' was the way one of her female colleagues at Classic Design had once described him.

Vivienne knew what she meant. Well over six feet tall, Jack possessed the same broad-shouldered, powerful body that you saw on wood-chopping champions. Just look what he'd done to her bathroom door! His face was all male as well, with a high forehead, strong nose, granite jaw and a wide, uncompromising mouth. Short dark hair and thick dark brows completed the macho picture.

There was no doubt a lot of women would find him quite attractive, despite his lack of warmth and charm. He did have nice blue eyes, Vivienne conceded, but they were usually hard and cold. They rarely twinkled with humour as they had a moment ago. Not that that made any difference to her. Jack was not her type and never would be.

For some reason, however, she couldn't help wondering just who *his* type of woman was. Who *did* he sleep with? When he could find the time, that was. It occurred to Vivienne that maybe he had a mistress stashed away somewhere who made herself available to him just for sex without expecting anything else. Except money, of course. Which Jack had plenty of.

Vivienne looked deep into his eyes, trying to see if he was that kind of man. His eyes didn't waver, boring back into hers, their expression no longer amused. A strangely erotic shiver ran down Vivienne's spine as she realised that, yes, he probably would have a mistress. How odd, she thought, that she would find such an arrangement rather titillating. She should have been disgusted. But she wasn't. Not even remotely.

'You've gone very quiet all of a sudden,' Jack said, breaking into her somewhat shocked silence.

'Sorry. Just thinking. I've been doing a lot of thinking today. That was what I was doing in the bath all that time—thinking.' After which she'd listened to music, some very loud, mind-numbing music. Hence her not hearing anyone knocking on the bathroom door.

'Not much to be gained by too much thinking,' Jack said. '*Doing* is the solution to most of life's problems. You need to keep busy, Vivienne. Whether it's working for me or someone else is immaterial. But you need to do something, not just sit around, not eating and not sleeping whilst your mind torments you with depressing thoughts. Next thing you know you'll be stuffing yourself with pills every day, weeks will go by and before you know it you'll be unemployable.'

'Oh dear… From the sounds of things, it wasn't just Nigel telling tales but Marion as well.'

'They only have your best interests at heart, Vivienne.'

'And you, Jack? Do you only have my best interests at heart by offering me this job?'

He shrugged. 'I have to confess your best interests weren't my first priority when I came here today. But that doesn't mean I'm totally heartless. Trust me when I say that one day you'll be glad that you didn't marry that bastard.'

Vivienne's teeth clenched hard in her jaw at Jack's possibly well-meaning but still wounding words. She'd loved Daryl and it would take her longer than one miserable month to get over his betrayal.

At the same time, she wasn't about to crawl into a

hole and let him destroy her entirely. Jack was right. She did still have her work.

'Perhaps,' she bit out. 'All right, run your proposal by me and I'll see what I think.'

Five minutes later, Vivienne had to admit that Jack had surprised her. And also intrigued her. The last thing she would have expected him to want her services for was to do a complete refurbishment of a holiday home he'd bought out in the bush. Well, not the bush exactly. Port Stephens was on the coast not that far north of Newcastle, which was the second biggest city in New South Wales and not too long a drive from Sydney— two and a half, maybe three hours.

Because of its location, Port Stephens had become a popular holiday and retirement area. Vivienne had never been there herself, but she'd seen a segment about the area on a travel programme not long ago. Whilst the beaches and bays did look spectacular, and the various townships dotted along the coast perfectly civilised, there was still a lot of rugged bush around. Not only that; from what Jack told her, the house he'd bought wasn't a typical beach shack sitting just off the sand. It did have water views but it was set back in the hills, and was simply huge, with a décor that was a mad mixture of Mediterranean villa and a fifties Hollywood mansion.

All in all, Francesco's Folly sounded fascinating, and would no doubt be a challenge to fix up. A distracting and consuming challenge which would take ages. Just what she needed right now.

'I have to admit you've surprised me,' she said.

Jack leant back in his chair. 'But are you interested in doing the job?'

'Absolutely,' she said in a firm voice.

'Now *you've* surprised *me*,' Jack admitted. 'I was sure you were going to say no.'

Vivienne shrugged. 'I only said I was interested, Jack. I haven't said a definite yes yet.'

'Fair enough.' Jack glanced at his watch then up into her face, his blue eyes no longer twinkling with humour. He was back to business. 'Look, I don't know about you, but I'm starving. Marion said you don't have much food in this place so I suggest you get yourself dressed and we'll go find a local restaurant. We can work out the details of the job over lunch. I can't actually sign you up till contracts have been exchanged on the property, but that shouldn't take long. I rang my solicitor last night and told him to hurry things through. Meanwhile, I'm sure the estate agent handling the sale will be only too happy to give us the keys so that you can look through the place. I'll drive you up there tomorrow.'

'Tomorrow!' Vivienne exclaimed.

'What's wrong with tomorrow? Don't tell me you have anything else you have to do, because we both know you haven't.'

Vivienne suppressed a sigh. She supposed it was too much to ask Jack to act any differently than he usually did when he was on site, charging through each minute of the day like he was perpetually on a deadline. If the man did have a mistress, she could just imagine how his visits to her would go. He'd ring her in advance and tell her to get her gear off so that she could be ready to service him the second he walked in the door.

Once again, Vivienne was shocked that she found such a scenario perversely exciting. Shocked that her body thought so too, her belly and nipples tightening underneath her robe. Thank the Lord it was a thick fluffy robe which hid everything. But her cheeks still flushed slightly as a wave of heat raced involuntarily through her veins. Her teeth immediately clenched down hard in her jaw as she battled for control over her mind, and her uncharacteristically wayward flesh. Vivienne wasn't used to being sexually excited by her thoughts. She'd always needed romance to turn her on. And a man she was in love with.

Her immediate somewhat panicky response was to tell Jack that she wasn't hungry and he should go get himself something to eat then come back later. But then Vivienne decided she was being silly. Jack didn't know her secret thoughts, or feelings. On top of that, she *was* hungry.

'Well, go on,' Jack ordered. 'Go and get dressed.'

Vivienne rolled her eyes but still stood up and headed for her bedroom, hopeful that the irritation Jack's bossy manner always evoked in her would douse the unexpected heat he'd been somehow generating. Not that it was him exactly who'd been turning her on: it had been her imaginings over his mistress, the one who probably didn't even exist. Why she'd invented her, Vivienne had no idea. But she vowed to put her and what Jack did with her right out of her head.

But typically that was easier said than done. As she put on her underwear—white cotton bikini briefs and a white stretchy bra, which minimised rather than enhanced her double-D-cup breasts—Vivienne started wondering what kind of underwear mistresses wore. Something very sexy, no doubt. Nothing made of cotton, that was for sure. Or possibly nothing at all.

'Oh God!' Vivienne cried, and dropped her head into her hands.

CHAPTER FOUR

JACK ANSWERED FIVE missed calls, arranged for a man to come and look at Vivienne's bathroom door tomorrow and booked them a table for a late lunch in the time it took Vivienne to make her reappearance, dressed in bone-coloured slacks, a white T-shirt and a black linen jacket. Her hair was still down and she was wearing only a minimum of make-up, especially around her eyes, which were bloodshot and red-rimmed.

'You've been crying,' he said stupidly before he could think better of it.

Vivienne shot him a droll look. 'No kidding. It's what women do when the man they love turns out to be a two-timing rat. I'm sorry, Jack, but if you want me to work for you in the coming weeks you'll have to risk being on the end of a few crying jags.'

'Fine,' he said. 'As long as you don't expect me to do anything about them.'

She looked taken aback. 'Like what?'

'I have two sisters and a mother,' he informed Vivienne. 'If I didn't hug them when they cried in front of me—which is depressingly often—I would be banned from their lives for ever.'

'You have two sisters and a mother?'

Jack laughed at the astonished expression on her

face. 'What did you think—that I was a foundling, abandoned on a building site when I was a few days old?'

She smiled. She actually smiled. Not a common trait of Vivienne's. She was one serious girl.

'Not quite,' she said. 'But you don't come across as a man in touch with his feminine side.'

'Then you'd be wrong. Living with three women for a good chunk of my life meant I had no choice. Though it was more *their* feminine side I had to be in touch with rather than my own. I have to confess I'm not the kind of guy who cooks and cleans and sends soppy cards, but I do hugs very well.'

'And you bring the right flowers, when required.'

Jack wasn't sure if she was being sarcastic or witty.

'Which I haven't thanked you for,' she went on with seeming sincerity. 'Sorry, Jack. It's not like me to be rude. Or ungrateful. I guess I'm not myself at the moment.'

'Apology accepted. Now, shall we get out of here? Time's marching on and I've booked us a table for lunch.'

She blinked. 'You have? Where?'

'Why don't I just surprise you again?'

He certainly did surprise Vivienne again, in more ways than one. Not only by taking her to a very trendy seafood restaurant which overlooked nearby Balmoral Beach, but by the way he was treated there by the staff—like he was an extremely valued client who deserved the very best table and the very best service. Which he definitely got, with drinks brought and their orders taken in no time flat.

Clearly, Jack had been there more than once, which gave rise to the speculation that he might not be as much of a workaholic as she'd imagined him to be. Maybe he did have an active social life. And a proper girlfriend as opposed to a mistress. Not that she would ever ask such a personal question. Not directly.

But a certain amount of curiosity got the better of Vivienne in the end.

'I gather you come here often?' she said casually as she lifted her glass of mineral water to her lips. She'd declined his offer of wine. If she started drinking, she might become maudlin again.

'Often enough,' he replied noncommittally. 'My mother lives on that hill over there. She loves seafood so I usually bring her here at least once a month. We also came here this year for Mother's Day. The rest of the family came too. Given both my sisters are now married with children, we had to book a seriously large table.'

'I see,' Vivienne said, then decided, what the heck? She wanted to know more. 'And you, Jack—why aren't you married with children?'

It was a reasonable enough question and he didn't seem to mind her asking, judging by his nondescript expression.

'If I said I never had the time, or the energy, you probably wouldn't believe me. But it's true. My dad died when I was seventeen, leaving the family in terrible debt. I had to leave school and get to work straight away. I wasn't happy, I can tell you; I'd made plans to go to uni to become an engineer. But that quickly went by the board. Still, I'm not complaining about that. I made good with what I did.'

'You certainly did,' Vivienne agreed. 'Your company is not only successful, it's one of the few construction companies in Sydney with a reputation for finishing projects on budget, on time *and* with good workmanship.'

Jack smiled at her. 'You forgot to mention that I hire only the best in the business as well, which includes interior designers.'

'And you forgot to mention why, after you made good, you still didn't have time for marriage and children. Let's face it, Jack, you've been at the top of the building ladder for some time now.'

'True. But getting there was a hard slog. Then there was the responsibility of looking after my two younger sisters and my mother. My mother in particular. Mum's not the strongest woman, emotionally. After my dad died, she totally fell apart. Even now, she has a tendency to fall into a depression at the drop of a hat. Some people are like that, you know. It's hard on them and hard on the people who love them and care about them.'

'Yes,' Vivienne said with more empathy than he could possibly realise. 'I'm sure it is.'

'It's a difficult situation to understand unless you live it,' he said, assuming—mistakenly—that she wasn't personally acquainted with such problems. 'Anyway, like I said, by the time I was making serious money I just didn't want to take on any further commitments or responsibilities. I still don't. I… Hell, Vivienne,' he broke off suddenly, his blue eyes startled. 'Why on earth am I telling you all this?'

Vivienne rolled her eyes. Truly, anyone would think he'd committed a crime by unburdening his soul a bit. At least he had one. Unlike some people!

'For pity's sake, Jack,' she said, a little more sharply than she intended. 'Don't go all "macho male" on me. There's no harm in expressing your feelings occasionally. Women do it all the time. You should hear Marion and me when we have a girls' night out. If you must know, I think it's sweet the way you've looked after your family, especially your mother. As for your not wanting marriage and children… Well, there's nothing wrong with that either. You have the right to live your life as you see fit. I was just curious. After all, you're quite a catch. I dare say you've had loads of women running after you over the years.'

'I've had my moments of being targeted.' He opened his mouth to say something more then shut it again. Vivienne was wondering what he'd been about to say when their meals arrived—his and hers lobsters, along with French fries and side salads.

'Oh my God,' she said with a groan as she salivated over the food. 'I didn't realise till this very moment just how hungry I was.'

'You and me both. Come on, let's stop with the chit-chat and tuck in.'

Tuck in they did, all conversation ceasing as they went about the all-consuming task of totally stuffing their faces. Vivienne gave the occasional satisfied sigh whilst Jack did nothing but crunch and munch. It wasn't until there wasn't a morsel of succulent flesh left on her lobster that Vivienne lifted her head, only to find that Jack had just finished his lobster as well and was licking his fingertips with relish.

No, not licking. *Sucking.*

'That was seriously good,' he said between somewhat noisy sucks.

Vivienne didn't say a word. Because she was staring at what Jack was doing and having the most inappropriate thoughts about his fingers. His amazingly long, thick fingers…

When a decidedly kinky fantasy involving herself

and Jack filled her head, Vivienne sat up straight, pressing her spine hard against the back of the chair. She was totally rattled, not just by the erotic nature of her thoughts, but by the way her muscles had tightened deep inside her, as though in anticipation of being invaded by Jack's fingers. She took several deep, calming breaths whilst she struggled to make sense of her behaviour. This was the second time that day that Jack had somehow turned her on. Not consciously, of course. Or deliberately. He would have no idea what mad thoughts he'd been evoking, first about his having a mistress stashed away somewhere, and now about his doing seriously intimate things to her with his fingers.

She wondered dazedly if her focus on things sexual had something to do with Daryl leaving her. Vivienne had been plagued over the past month by thoughts that she hadn't satisfied him in bed, despite his always having said that she did. She'd wondered, during her think-fest in the bath, if Courtney Ellison did kinky things to Daryl that he'd always secretly craved, and which he now couldn't live without. Maybe her own weird behaviour today was a rebound or a revenge thing, a crazy desire to prove to herself that she could be as wildly sexual as any woman.

Whatever, Vivienne could not deny that she was turned on at this moment. If only Jack would stop sucking those damned fingers!

She turned her eyes away, then did what she always did when life threatened to overwhelm her: she concentrated on work.

'So, Jack,' she said, looking back at him with her business face on. 'Tell me exactly what the terms of my employment will be.'

Jack frowned as he picked up his white linen serviette and wiped his fingertips.

'I can't really give you specifics yet,' he said. 'Not till I see the place again. If you come with me tomorrow, you can inspect Francesco's Folly for yourself and tell me how long you think the job will take to complete. I always prefer to pay designers a lump sum rather than so much per hour. At the same time, given you would be doing me a special favour by taking this job, I am prepared to be generous.'

Vivienne's eyebrows lifted. Jack Stone was not known for his generosity. He was a fair businessman, but tough.

'*How* generous?' she asked.

'*Very* generous.'

'But why? I'm sure you could get any number of up-and-coming young designers to do the job for next to nothing. It would be a feather in their cap.'

'But I don't want any other up-and-coming designer, Vivienne. I want *you*.'

CHAPTER FIVE

WHEN JACK SAID he wanted Vivienne, he'd meant it as a strictly professional statement, the same one he'd made to Nigel earlier that day.

But as he looked deep into her gorgeous green eyes—eyes which had widened slightly at his words— the thought hit Jack that he didn't want Vivienne just professionally, but physically as well.

It was a stunning realisation, one which left Jack speechless. After all, not until today had he seriously fancied Vivienne. Okay, so he'd been aware of her good looks, and had occasionally given her a second glance as she'd walked by.

But she'd never given him a hard-on. Not once.

Yet she'd already done that twice today. Once, when he'd seen her naked in the bath, and right now, here, in this restaurant.

It was this second unexpected erection which totally threw him, because there was nothing happening which should have stirred lust in him: no nakedness; no flirtation. Hell, they were just discussing business.

But lust was very much in control of Jack's body at that moment. *And* his mind. Effortlessly, it stripped Vivienne of her clothes until she was naked before him, the mental image of her sitting there in the nude bringing his arousal to an almost painful level.

God in heaven, he thought frustratedly, *what on earth am I going to do now?*

Absolutely nothing, he decided ruefully. Because there was nothing he *could* do. To make a play for Vivienne in her present emotionally charged and highly vulnerable state was both unconscionable and extremely unlikely to be productive.

But what of later? he wondered. The job he'd asked her to do would take weeks. No, probably months. Could he wait that long before making his move? Probably not, if the bulge in his jeans was anything to go by. Hopefully, it wasn't Vivienne herself sparking all this urgent desire, but his long stint of celibacy.

'But *why* do you want me?' Vivienne persisted.

Jack hoped his face didn't betray the thoughts which immediately ran through his head. Because they had nothing to do with work.

'Why? Because you're seriously good,' he replied, all the while wishing that she wasn't. At this moment, he wished she were seriously bad. The Courtney Ellison type of bad. If that were the case, the possibilities were endless.

The waiter arrived fortuitously at that moment, sweeping away their plates and asking them if they wanted dessert. Vivienne declined. So did Jack, briskly ordering them coffee instead. By the time they were alone again, he'd managed to stop the X-rated images bombarding his brain, his conscience castigating him at the same time for reducing a nice girl like Vivienne to little more than a sex object.

Vivienne was seriously glad that the waiter arrived when he did, stopping her from making a fool of herself

by asking more stupid questions as to why Jack wanted
her specifically for the job. What had she been expecting him to say, for pity's sake? She already knew that
he liked her work. He'd said so on many occasions. Had
she been looking for more praise? More ego-stroking?
Or something else—something which she hardly dared
admit, even to herself…

When another embarrassing wave of sexual heat
started flowing through Vivienne's body, she stood up
so abruptly that her chair almost tipped over backwards.
She grabbed it just in time, throwing Jack a weak smile
as she excused herself and headed for the rest room.

It was a flushed and confused Vivienne who leant
on the washstand and stared into the wall mirror above
the twin basins. Lord, what was happening to her here?
First, she'd entertained kinky fantasies involving Jack's
fingers, then she'd started hoping he'd say he wanted her
and her only for the job because he wanted *her*. Which
was even crazier, considering any female with a brain
in her head knew when a man fancied her. And Jack
didn't. Never had. The same way she'd never fancied
him. Until today, that was. Suddenly, she seemed to be
finding him extremely attractive. No, not just attractive—sexy. Dead sexy.

The logical part of Vivienne's mind told her this definitely had something to do with Daryl leaving her. His
desertion had unhinged her and she'd become desperate. Desperate for someone, if not to love her, than at
least to want her. Women sometimes did stupid things
after being dumped. A girlfriend of hers had once cut
her hair very short and bleached it white. Another had
gone out and had a boob job. A third had slept with a
different man every night for a month. You didn't reach

the age of twenty-seven without having witnessed a few of your female friends lose the plot over men.

Vivienne had no intention of cutting her hair. Or of going blonde. Or having a boob job. Neither was she about to cruise bars every night in search of one-night stands. But she was awfully tempted—awfully, *awfully* tempted—to try to make Jack Stone want her for more than redecorating Francesco's Folly. She wanted him to look at her with fire in those hard blue eyes of his. Wanted him to want her so badly that he'd stop at nothing to have her.

Vivienne shook her head, her shoulders slumping. Who was she kidding? None of that was ever going to happen. She wasn't the kind of girl who could turn a man's head against his will. She wasn't a flirt, let alone a *femme fatale*. Before Daryl, she'd had less than a handful of lovers. She was, if truth be told, on the shy side when it came to bedroom matters. Daryl had been the one to pursue her, to seduce her, to make her fall in love with him.

Vivienne frowned at this last thought. Was that true? Had Daryl somehow *made* her fall in love with him? How odd that sounded, as though she hadn't had any choice. If there was one thing Vivienne was proud of, it was her ability to make choices in life. To decide. That was what she'd been doing in the bath today—deciding what to do with the rest of her life. Not that she'd come to any solid conclusion in the matter. She'd still been too upset to think rationally. In the end, she'd just lain back in the warm water and listened to music, unaware of time passing and the water cooling.

Jack breaking down the door had shocked the life out of her, not to mention seriously embarrassed her. She hadn't enjoyed his getting an eyeful of her bare breasts.

An exhibitionist, she was not! Which made her subse-
quent sexual responses to him even harder to fathom.
None of it made any sense at all!

When another woman came into the rest room Vivienne scurried into one of the cubicles where, with a bit
of luck, she could sit and think in peace. She hated not
being able to think clearly.

*So what are you going to do about this job offer from
Jack, Vivienne?* came that stern voice that would pop up
in her head on the rare occasions she began to waffle
over something. *You don't have to do it. He can't force
you. Come on, girl, make a decision!*

Vivienne gnawed at her bottom lip as she considered
the pros and cons.

To knock him back would not be the best of moves
work-wise, if she wanted to continue being a designer.
Jack was a powerful man in the building industry. At
the same time, it was going to be awkward, being alone
with him in the car tomorrow and then working with
him on such a personal project. No doubt they would
have to spend more time together than when she usually
worked for him. Not an enjoyable situation, if she kept
being besieged by hot thoughts about him all the time.

But what was her alternative? Say no and stay home,
wallowing in her misery? Vivienne shuddered at the
thought. She supposed she could pack her bags and go
on a holiday somewhere. But she would still be alone.
Alone and unhappy, with nothing to distract her. She'd
rather take back her resignation and return to work for
Classic Design than do that. Running away never solved
anything. You had to face things in life. Face reality!

*Okay, so face it, Vivienne! For some weird and won-
derful reason today, you're madly attracted to Jack.*

Madly attracted and seriously turned on. That's the truth of the matter.

But there's absolutely no basis for this sudden attraction, she argued with herself. Jack wasn't even her type, physically. Vivienne had always found big men intimidating, not appealing at all.

Maybe it was just a temporary aberration. Maybe she'd wake up tomorrow and these mad feelings would be gone. Maybe when she saw him in the morning, she'd only feel what she used to feel for him. Which was a mixture of irritation and exasperation at his bossy ways and less than charming manner.

Soothed by such sensible reasoning, Vivienne decided not to make a hasty decision. She'd wait and see what happened tomorrow. If the drive up there with Jack was a nightmare of frustration and confusion, she'd decline his offer, saying she was sorry but she simply wasn't up to such a big job at this time.

Surely Jack would understand?

It was a relief to find, as she made her way back to their table, that when she looked over at him, sitting there drumming his index finger on the white linen tablecloth, her only feelings were wry ones. He really was a most impatient man. Impatient, demanding and not happy, unless things were going his way.

Remembering this, Vivienne conceded Jack probably wouldn't react well if she rejected his proposal. No doubt he would argue with her then offer her more money, neither of which would work. If he knew her better, he'd know she couldn't be bullied, or bribed into anything she didn't want to do.

But maybe it wouldn't come to that. Clearly, she was already over what had taken possession of her earlier.

Her brain was now crystal clear and firmly in control of her body.

'Coffee not here yet?' she said politely as she pulled out her chair and sat down.

'Nope. So, is it a yes or a no, Vivienne? Give it to me straight.'

Vivienne almost smiled. Oh yes, things were right back to normal. But she still wasn't about to be bullied into saying yes prematurely.

'I think, Jack, that it would be wise for me not to commit myself till I see Francesco's Folly in person.'

'Okay, I'll pick you up early tomorrow morning. Around seven. So don't go taking too many of those sleeping tablets the doctor gave you.'

Vivienne gave an exasperated sigh. 'Marion's a good friend but she talks too much. What else did she tell you about me?'

'Not much. She did say that you owned rather than rented your apartment. But that was only because I asked her. She didn't volunteer the information.'

'I see. And why did you want to know that?' she asked, thinking to herself that he'd probably been trying to gauge her financial situation. Knowledge was power, after all.

'No good reason. It surprised me, that's all, how starkly furnished the place was. It didn't have your signature warmth and style.'

'Oh,' she said, taken aback that he would notice. Her chest tightened as it did whenever she thought of the reasons why her apartment was the way it was. You couldn't explain something like that. When Marion had asked her the same thing, she'd just said she hated clutter. Of course, it went deeper than that. Much, much deeper.

'I haven't long had the apartment renovated,' she said. 'The decorating's not finished yet.'

'Ah. That explains it, then. I thought maybe the boyfriend had taken some things with him when he left.'

Vivienne rather liked the disdain with which Jack said 'the boyfriend' rather than Daryl's name.

'Daryl didn't own anything,' she bit out. 'Only his clothes.' And she'd bought most of them. His salary as a mobile phone salesman didn't extend to trendy designer wear. God, but she'd been a fool where that man was concerned. Quite unconsciously her right hand went to the fourth finger on her left hand, where her engagement ring had resided until a month ago.

She'd bought that, too, Daryl having promised faithfully that he would pay her back.

But he never had.

Currently, it was languishing in the top drawer of her bedside table, a visual testament to her stupidity.

Vivienne realised suddenly that Courtney Ellison must have paid for the rock she'd been proudly displaying in those photographs published in the gossip section of last Sunday's paper. No way could Daryl have afforded a diamond that size, not unless it was a fake one. Actually, it wouldn't surprise her if it *was* a fake diamond. A fake diamond to go with his fake persona.

The coffee arrived at that point, in a silver pot, along with a jug of cream and a plate full of after-dinner mints. The waiter poured the coffee then left them to do the rest. Vivienne added cream and two cubes of sugar to hers. Jack left his black.

'He didn't leave you because of *you*, Vivienne,' he said abruptly after taking a sip of his coffee. 'It was because of the fortune he stands to inherit as Courtney's husband.'

Vivienne gritted her teeth before looking up. 'Maybe.'

Marion had said the same thing, and of course the logical part of Vivienne agreed with her. But she still couldn't get it out of her head that somehow she was at fault as well. Perhaps Daryl had got sick of her obsession with tidiness, not to mention her sexual inhibitions. She wasn't keen on oral sex, or adventurous positions where she felt exposed and vulnerable. Even being on top bothered her. Daryl had always said that he didn't need her to do any of that stuff if she didn't want to; that making love to *her* was enough for him.

'No sane man would leave a nice girl like you for a woman like Courtney Ellison,' Jack said. 'Not unless the carrot was gold-plated.'

Vivienne might have been flattered, if the thought hadn't struck her that if Daryl was such a cold-blooded fortune hunter then he'd probably pursued *her* because of her money. She might not be in Courtney Ellison's financial league but she wasn't poor either. She owned her own apartment and car, and still had a substantial bank balance. On top of that, as one of Sydney's most successful young designers, she earned a six-figure salary.

The conclusion that Daryl had *never* loved her, that their relationship had been nothing but a con from the start, was even more shattering than his leaving her.

When Jack saw Vivienne's face go ashen, he decided a quick change of subject was called for.

'Before I forget,' he said as he plonked his coffee cup back onto its saucer. 'The chap I've organised to come look at your bathroom door will be at your place the same time as me—seven. Not that he can fix it on the spot. When I told him the door would need replacing, not repairing, he said he'd have to take measurements to make sure he got the right door.'

Vivienne made a scoffing sound. 'And you trust a tradesman to arrive on time? When I had my apartment renovated I soon discovered that tradies have a totally different time schedule to the rest of the world.'

'Then you should have called in my company to do the work,' Jack said. 'Trust me when I tell you the carpenter I've booked will be at your door bang on seven. He knows that if he's late I won't be hiring him again.'

'I'll have to see it to believe it.'

'Then you will. I'll be on time, too. Just make sure you're up and ready.'

'You don't have to worry about me,' came her rueful reply. 'I'm nothing if not punctual.'

Jack frowned at the underlying depression in her words, anger quickly joining his concern. That bastard had done a real number on Vivienne's self-esteem. If he ever came across him again, he'd flatten him, and to hell with the consequences!

'You sound tired,' he said. 'Come on; drink up your coffee and I'll take you home. I can see you're in need of some serious sleep.'

Vivienne opened her mouth to tell him that he wasn't her boss—yet—so he could stop with the orders. But then she realised that he was only trying to be kind. He just didn't know any other way but bossy and controlling. So she drank her coffee and let him drive her home. Once there, she declined his offer to walk her to the door, but he just ignored her and did it anyway. Vivienne decided not to argue. She was beyond arguing.

'Are you sure you'll be all right?' Jack asked as she went about slowly inserting her key into the lock.

She sighed as she turned and glanced up at him. 'I'll be fine,' she said somewhat wearily. 'Thanks for the very nice lunch, Jack. I did thank you for the flowers before, didn't I?'

'Yes.'

'Good. I'm not quite all there at the moment.'

'I can see that. But you'll be better tomorrow. And even better the day after that.'

'I certainly hope so.'

'I *know* so. All you have to do is do what Dr Jack tells you. Till tomorrow morning, then,' he said, giving Vivienne no warning before his head bent to deliver a goodbye peck.

It was just a platonic kiss but, when his lips made contact with hers, Vivienne's heart stopped beating altogether. Thank God he spun away immediately and strode off without a backward glance. Because if he'd looked down into her face after lifting his head he would have seen something not so platonic in her eyes.

'Crazy,' she said with another sigh. 'I'm definitely going crazy.'

CHAPTER SIX

'I'M A BLOODY idiot,' Jack muttered to himself as he jumped into his car, slammed it into gear and accelerated away.

He knew he should go back to the office. There was always work to be done. Instead, he drove back down to Balmoral Beach where he turned off his mobile phone then sat in his car for a ridiculously long time, thinking. Then, when he couldn't stand trying to work things out in his head a moment longer, he did something even more futile: he drove to his mother's house.

She was home, of course. His mother was always home nowadays, recently having added agoraphobia to her long list of anxiety disorders. The only time she'd been out of the house during the past year was on Mother's Day, and for her birthday back in February. Jack had tried to get her to go to Vanuatu with him in March but to no avail.

'Jack!' she exclaimed when she opened the front door, looking surprisingly well, he noted. *And* very nicely dressed. Sometimes, when he came to visit, he found her still in her dressing gown in the middle of the day. 'It's not like you to visit on a weekday,' she added. 'There's nothing wrong, is there?'

'Nope,' he lied. No point in telling his mother about

his personal problems. It would only upset her. 'I was in the area for work and decided to pop in and see you.'

'How nice. Come in, then. Would you like some coffee?' she asked him as he followed her down to the kitchen.

'I won't say no,' he replied.

The kitchen was super-tidy today, he noted. His mother had always been a fastidious housekeeper when they'd been growing up, but after his father had died you could always tell how depressed she was by the state of her kitchen. Clearly, if the shining sink and bench-tops were anything to go by, his mother was far from depressed at the moment.

'You going out somewhere?' he asked as he sat down at the large wooden kitchen table.

His mother sent him a sheepish look from where she was standing by the kettle. 'Actually, yes, I am. But not till five. Jim next door—you know Jim, don't you?—has asked me out to dinner. We're going to a restaurant way up at Palm Beach. There aren't too many restaurants open on a Monday night, it seems.'

Jack could not hide his surprise that his mother would go out at all, let alone accept a date from a man.

'Yes, yes, I know,' she said. 'It's been a long time coming. But I finally got so sick of myself last week that I started talking to Jim over the fence when we were both outside gardening. We have spoken before, but only to say hello. Anyway, he was just so easy to talk to, and when he asked me over for a cup of tea I went. It was then that he asked me out to dinner and I said yes. I know he's a good few years older than me, but he's just so nice, and I thought, what have I got to lose by going out with him?'

'Absolutely nothing, Mum. I think it's great.'

'Do you?' she said as she brought his mug of black coffee over to the table. 'Do you really?' she repeated as she sat down opposite him.

'Of course. Jim's a decent man.' Jack had got to know Jim over the years his mother had lived in this house. He was always out in the garden and happy to have a word or two.

'I'm glad you approve. Because this isn't the first date I've had with him. We've been going out to dinner every night for almost a week.'

'Wow. No flies on Jim.'

When his mother blushed, the penny dropped.

'Wow again, Mum,' Jack said. 'And good for you. Good for you both, actually.'

'We don't want to get married,' his mother confided, her voice dropping to a conspiratorial whisper. 'We just want company.'

'I haven't seen you this happy in years,' he said.

Her blue eyes sparkled.

His mother astonished him further by lifting her chin and looking him straight in the eye. 'Now, I have to go put my make-up on, Jack. Stay and finish your coffee by all means but I would prefer it if you're gone by the time Jim comes to pick me up. I don't trust you not to say something embarrassing.'

'Who, me!' Jack exclaimed, doing his best to stop himself from smiling.

'Yes, you. You can be extremely tactless at times.'

'Who, *me*?' Now he was grinning widely.

'Oh for pity's sake,' she said, rolling her eyes at the same time. But she bent and kissed the top of his head. 'You're a good son and I love you dearly, but may I suggest you ring before you just pop in next time? I might have a visitor and I wouldn't want to shock you.'

It wasn't until Jack left the house ten minutes later that he stopped smiling and started thinking again. Not about his mother and Jim but about himself and Vivienne.

As he drove at a snail's pace back towards the city and home—rush-hour traffic had more than arrived—his thoughts ran over the events of the day, right up until that last moment when he'd kissed Vivienne goodbye. That had been the moment when it had hit home to him—with considerable force—that if he took Vivienne up to Francesco's Folly tomorrow there was a very real danger of his doing something which would spoil their working relationship for ever.

Jack didn't want that to happen. He valued Vivienne as a business colleague and respected her as a woman. But there was no denying that she'd stirred a lust in him today that was almost beyond reason. He'd imagined he'd got it under control back in the restaurant, but then he'd kissed her and all hell had broken loose.

'Worse than hell,' he muttered aloud, recalling how the second his lips had brushed over hers he'd been instantly besieged by the most violent urge to sweep her into his arms and kiss her properly. His struggle not to succumb to the temptation had almost exhausted his will power, so much so that he doubted he would be able to resist a second time.

Of course, he would not be stupid enough to kiss her a second time. That was a given. But it was still likely that he'd be plagued by ongoing thoughts about doing a lot more than just kissing her. Which would result in his getting turned on again.

Jack didn't want to spend tomorrow with a hard-on. So he guessed it was off to a club tonight, and sex with a virtual stranger.

Such a scenario would have excited him once upon a time. But no longer, it seemed. What Jack really wanted was to have great sex with a woman he knew and liked. A woman with gorgeous green eyes, long auburn hair and breasts to die for.

Jack banged his hands on the steering wheel, swearing in frustration.

His frustration grew all the way across the Harbour Bridge, reaching a furious peak by the time he let himself into his apartment. There, he stripped off all his clothes and jumped into a steaming hot shower. After a few minutes, he turned the tap abruptly to cold and stood there under the icy shards of water till his body was numb. Not so his brain, however. Nothing was going to rid his mind of the annoying reality that he wanted Vivienne as he had not wanted a woman in his entire life.

For a man who was used to achieving his goals, it exasperated Jack that he could not have what he wanted. If only he wasn't a modern man, he thought irritably, constrained by the rules of civilisation and society. Cave men had had it so much easier. If a cave man had seen a female he fancied, he'd just banged her on the head with a club then dragged her back to his cave, where he'd ravaged her silly, after which she'd become his woman.

Jack had to laugh at what would happen to him if he did that to Vivienne. He certainly wouldn't have to wait for the power of the law to punish him. She'd up and kill him the first chance she got. God, what he would not give to have her in his bed, not just once—once was not going to be *nearly* enough!—but on a regular basis.

By the time he'd exited the shower and wrapped a towel around himself, Jack had come to two decisions. One, he wasn't going to go pick up some stranger tonight. To hell with that idea! Two, he didn't care how long it took, or what he'd have to do to make it happen—one day, Vivienne Swan was going to be become his lover!

CHAPTER SEVEN

'THAT DIDN'T TAKE long, did it?' Jack said as he popped on his sunglasses then started up the powerful engine of his Porsche. 'I told you the door man would be on time.'

Vivienne gave him a cool smile in return before putting on her own sunglasses. After sleeping for fourteen hours straight, she'd woken at six this morning with a clear head and a determination to take control of her life once more—which included not falling apart over Daryl's lies, and not entertaining any further wanton thoughts about Jack Stone.

It was a still a relief, however, when he arrived and she was able to open the door to him without instantly wondering if he'd spent last night with his mistress, or whether other parts of his body were as big as his fingers. Yes, she did still find him more attractive than she had in the past. He looked *extremely* good in those tight blue jeans, white T-shirt and a navy zip-up jacket. But her thoughts didn't turn lustful, even when he bent over to show the door man the broken hinges.

Vivienne was also able to fold herself down into the low passenger seat of his sexy black sports car without worrying that being alone with him would prove too much for her. She felt rested and relaxed and almost back to her normal self. Thank heavens!

'I'll remember to call you the next time something goes wrong in my place and I need a tradie,' she said. 'You seem to have all the right contacts.'

'Call me any time you like,' he replied.

Vivienne frowned at the uncharacteristic warmth in his voice. She supposed he was just being nice so that she'd do the job he wanted her to do, the same way he'd been nice to her yesterday. But she seriously wished he'd go back to being as brusque and matter-of-fact as he usually was. That way, there'd be no chance of a repeat of what had happened to her yesterday.

'Do you mind if I ask you something personal?' he said.

Vivienne's frown deepened. '*How* personal?'

'It's about Daryl.'

'What about Daryl?'

'I only met him the once. Last year at your Christmas party. I've been puzzling over what was it about the man to make you fall in love with him?'

It startled Vivienne, that phrase Jack used about Daryl *making* her fall in love with him. For that was what she had thought herself: that somehow Daryl had *made* her fall in love with him.

'It sounds like you didn't like him much,' she said.

'You could say that.'

'But why? You only spoke to us that night for a few minutes.'

Jack shrugged. 'It doesn't take me long to form opinions of people.'

'In that case, what was your opinion?'

'He was a slick-talking, superficial charmer whom I wouldn't trust an inch.'

'Goodness! You really didn't like him, did you?'

'No, but obviously you did.'

'Well, yes…yes of course I did. I *loved* him.'

Jack liked the way she said that in the past tense. He liked also that his questions were making her think about the rotter she'd been planning to marry. He needed Vivienne to get over him fast. To move on with her life. Because that was his only chance of success with her in the near future.

Jack was not a patient man at the best of times. Seeing Vivienne again this morning had done little to dampen his desire for her, despite her wearing a rather androgynous black pants suit and having put her hair back up. He knew now what she looked like with her hair down, and what her breasts were like underneath that crisp, white schoolgirl blouse.

'But why, Vivienne?' he persisted. 'What was there to love about him? Surely it wasn't just because he was handsome?'

'No,' Vivienne denied, though Daryl *was* handsome. Very handsome. 'It was more the way he treated me.'

'You mean he said all the things you wanted to hear. Conmen are very good at lying, Vivienne. And giving compliments.'

'True,' Vivienne agreed. Daryl had paid her neverending compliments. Looking back, she could see that they had been over the top. She wasn't drop-dead gorgeous. Or *that* good a cook. And facing the evidence of her ex-fiancé's character was beginning to make her angry again. Though the anger this time was more directed at herself than him. How *could* she have been so stupid as to be taken in by that creep? What kind of idiot was she? It was some comfort that she hadn't finalised any arrangements for their wedding— as though deep down she'd known the wedding would never take place.

'Would you mind if we stopped talking about Daryl?' she said a bit sharply.

'Sorry,' Jack said. 'Do you want me to shut up altogether? It's just that it's a rather long drive. It could get a bit boring if we just sit here in silence. I could turn on the radio if you prefer, or put on some music. I have a flash stick with heaps of songs on it.'

'What kind of songs?' Vivienne asked, vowing to forget all about Daryl. He wasn't worth thinking about, anyway.

For a minute there, Jack had thought he'd made a big mistake, bringing up the subject of Vivienne's ex. She'd become very uptight with his questions. Clearly, she was still in love with the bastard. Or thought she was. It irked Jack that dear old Daryl had probably been great in bed. Men like that usually were. But what the heck? He wasn't too bad in the sack himself.

Jack felt confident that, if and when he managed to seduce Vivienne, she'd be happy enough in the morning. Not that he wanted actually to *seduce* Vivienne. Seduction suggested sneaky methods, such as excessive flattery, which had obviously been one of Daryl's tactics for getting a girl into bed. Jack had never learnt the art of flattery. He called a spade a spade. If he told a girl she was beautiful, it was because she *was* beautiful. Jack hated liars and manipulators, hated empty chit-chat as well. He was a doer, not a talker.

Or he usually was. It had come as a genuine surprise to him that he'd talked to Vivienne more yesterday than he'd ever talked to any woman. He'd even told her about his family background, and the problems he'd had with his mother. Which was a thought…

Jack decided not to bother with music for now and to stick to chit-chat.

'You'll never guess what my mother's gone and done,' he said.

Vivienne seemed momentarily taken aback by his sudden change of subject, her head whipping round to look at him.

'Er...no, I couldn't possibly guess. What?'

'She's having an affair with her next-door neighbour.'

'Heavens! I hope she's not best friends with his wife. That's not very nice.'

'No no, Jim's not married. Recently widowed.'

'Then it's not really an affair, is it? I mean, an affair suggests something illicit. Or secret.'

'True. Call it a fling, then. She's having a fling. They're not in love, or anything like that.'

'How do you know?'

'She said so. They're just good friends. And you know what? I've never seen her happier. Or more confident. I was somewhat shocked at first but, once I thought about it, I realised it was the best thing to happen to her in years.'

'So when did you find all this out?' Vivienne asked.

'Yesterday afternoon. I dropped in to see her after I left you.'

Jack was pleased when she smiled at him.

'You love her a lot, don't you? And worry about her a lot.'

'Mothers who live on their own can be a worry, especially ones who are on the emotionally fragile side.'

'Yes. Yes, that's so true.'

Jack detected a touch of irony in Vivienne's remark. Maybe her mother was a widow as well. Or divorced. But then he recalled Marion saying something about Vivienne inheriting some money recently. That usually meant a death in the family. But who? He would have to tread carefully. He didn't want her getting upset.

'You sound like you've had some personal experience with emotionally fragile mothers,' he said.

'Yes. Yes, I have, actually. Dad divorced Mum when she was still quite young and she never got over it. She died a couple of years ago. Heart attack,' Vivienne added, hoping it would stop Jack asking further questions about her mother's death. If she told him the truth it would be like opening Pandora's box, which she preferred to keep solidly closed.

'That's sad, Vivienne. And your father?'

'Oh, I haven't seen him since he walked out on Mum when I was about six. He went overseas and never came back.'

Jack's sidewards glance showed true shock. 'What kind of man would do something like that?'

Vivienne knew that there were excuses for her father's behaviour but to explain them would be delving into that Pandora's box again.

She shrugged. 'To give him credit, he did leave us well provided for. He gave Mum everything they'd accumulated during their ten-year marriage: the house. The furniture. Two cars. And he paid child support for me till I was eighteen.'

'And so he should have!' Jack said, clearly outraged. 'He should also have kept in touch. Been a proper father to you. I presume it was just you, Vivienne? Sounds like you don't have any other brothers or sisters.'

'No. There was just me,' she said, her chest tightening with the effort of staying calm in the face of memories which were better kept buried.

Jack shook his head. 'It never ceases to amaze me how some men can just walk away and turn their backs on their families, especially their children. Why have children if you're not going to love and care for them? Bloody hell, did you see that?' he growled, thumping the steering wheel at the same time. 'That stupid idiot in that four-wheel drive almost took my front off.'

Vivienne was extremely grateful that that stupid idiot in the four-wheel drive had interrupted what was becoming an increasingly awkward conversation, giving her the opportunity to deflect Jack's attention onto other less painful subjects.

'So how long do you think it will take us to get to Port Stephens?' she asked.

'Mmm. Let's see… It's going on eight and we're about to turn onto the motorway. It took me two and half hours last Sunday from here, but I didn't stop anywhere.'

'You don't have to stop anywhere for me,' Vivienne said. 'I'll be fine. I had a big bowl of porridge for breakfast which usually keeps me going till lunchtime.'

Jack's eyebrows lifted. 'Fancy that. I had porridge too. And you're right. It does stick to your ribs. But I think we might still have a coffee break at Raymond Terrace.'

'I'm not sure where that is. I haven't been up this way before.'

'Really?'

'To tell the truth, I haven't done much travelling of any kind. Never even been out of Australia.' Or Sydney, for that matter, she didn't add. No point in courting more awkward questions.

'I haven't travelled all that much, either,' Jack replied. 'If and when I do take a break, it's to places that it doesn't take long to fly to, like Bali or Vanuatu and Fiji. You know me—busy, busy, busy.'

'Maybe it's time you slowed down a bit.'

'I couldn't agree with you more. That's one of the reasons I bought Francesco's Folly.'

'Francesco's Folly,' Vivienne repeated thoughtfully. 'Do you know why it was called that?'

'The estate agent said Francesco was the name of the Italian who built the place back in the late seventies. The folly part will be self-explanatory once you see the place. I gather our Italian had a large family, most of whom he outlived. He finally passed away a couple of months ago at the age of ninety-five. His two great-grandsons inherited the place but they both live in Queensland and wanted it sold, pronto. Which is where I came in.'

'I can't wait to see it,' Vivienne said.

'And I can't wait to show it to you,' Jack replied.

CHAPTER EIGHT

IT TOOK THEM longer than anticipated to reach Port Stephens, stopping for over half an hour on the Pacific Highway just north of Newcastle. Jack answered several missed business calls and Vivienne had a nice long chat with Marion, who was pleased to hear that her friend was feeling better and planning to get back to work, though not necessarily with Classic Design.

After leaving Raymond Terrace, it took them a good forty minutes to drive to Nelson's Bay—the main seaside town in Port Stephens—where they picked up the keys from the agency handling the property, then made their way to Francesco's Folly, which was near an area called Soldier's Point. Despite having enjoyed the drive and the scenery, by the time Jack turned his Porsche into the driveway of their destination, Vivienne was keen to see the house.

And what a house it was! Only two storeyed, but it looked like a mansion perched up on top of a hill. Mediterranean in style, it was cement-rendered in a salmon-pink colour and had more archways and columns than Vivienne had seen outside of a convent or a museum.

'Heavens to Betsy!' Vivienne exclaimed as Jack drove up the long, extremely steep driveway.

Jack grinned over at her. 'It's pretty spectacular, isn't it?'

'Not quite a traditional Aussie holiday house, I have to admit. A mad mixture of Tuscan villa and Greek palace. What's it like inside?'

'Extremely dated. Trust me when I say you'll have your work cut out for you to transform it into something I could live with on a permanent basis. But the views, Vivienne. The views are to die for.'

'But Jack, it's enormous!' she said as they drew closer and she began to appreciate the true proportions of the place. 'Are you sure you want to buy a place this size? I mean…it would be different if you were married with a big family, like Francesco was.'

Jack shrugged. 'I have two married sisters with a total of five children between them. And a mother with a lover. They'll use the place, too. Though, to be brutally honest, I'm not buying it for them. I'm buying it for myself.

'I knew the moment I walked out onto one of those balconies up there that I wanted to live here,' he said, pointing to the balconies, which spanned the full length of both floors. 'Maybe not twenty-four-seven just yet, but at least at weekends and for holidays. Call me crazy if you like but that's the way it is. Now, stop trying to talk me out of this, Vivienne,' he said as they drove round to the back of the house. 'It's a done deal.'

The back of the house was where the garages were located, along with the main entrance to the house, guarded by two huge brass doors with equally huge brass locks. The tarred driveway also gave way to a gravel courtyard, the wheels of the Porsche making crunching noises as Jack brought his car to a halt in front of the multiple garages.

'Leave that behind,' Jack ordered when she picked

up her bag. 'I don't want us being interrupted by phone calls. I'll leave my phone behind as well.'

'What about my camera?' she asked. 'I'd like to take photos.'

'No photos first up. Just your eyes. Come on.'

She did as ordered, despite thinking to herself that if she agreed to do this job she would have to learn to bite her tongue a lot. Jack really was a control freak, in her humble opinion. She smiled a wry smile when he made her stand back while he unlocked the brass doors and pushed them wide open, after which he turned and stood, still barring her way.

'Now, before you call me a liar,' he said. 'This first part of the house is not too bad.'

Vivienne almost laughed when she walked inside. 'Not too bad' was a serious understatement! The foyer alone was quite magnificent with a vaulted ceiling and an Italian-marble floor, an elegantly curved staircase on each side leading up to the first floor. Straight ahead was a wide columned archway, beyond which lay a huge indoor swimming pool, which seemingly stretched for ever, before running under another columned archway and ending out in the sunshine.

'Wow,' was all she could think of to say.

'Yes. The pool is Hollywood wow,' Jack agreed. 'Not solar heated, however, something which I would want to have done. But that wouldn't be your problem. Yours is the décor of the rooms, which are many and varied.

'On each side of the pool there's a self-contained three-bedroomed apartment,' he explained as he took Vivienne's hand and led her along the left side of the pool. 'In recent years, Francesco used to let them out in the summer. But that was before he became ill. After that, he just lived upstairs, the downstairs apartments were left empty and the whole place became run down.'

'It doesn't look that run down,' Vivienne said, trying to keep her focus on her surrounds and not on her hand in Jack's. Lord, but she wished she could extract her hand without such a move being rude, but before she could do so his fingers tightened around hers. Her breath caught as a violently electric current raced up her arm and down through her entire body, tightening her nipples and belly on the way.

So much for her having this insane sexual attraction under control!

'I gather the estate agent got in a team of cleaners before the place was opened for inspection,' Jack said as he walked on, a totally rattled Vivienne in tow. 'The great-grandsons took away what furniture they wanted, so all the rooms are half-empty, which perhaps didn't serve the sellers well. It highlighted how neglected everything was and I was able to negotiate a bargain. But enough of that for now. Come and see the view.'

Thankfully, he let go of her hand once they reached the sun-drenched balcony, and Vivienne was quick to put some distance between herself and Jack, walking swiftly over to stand at the iron railing, which she gripped with both hands as though her life depended on it. And it did, actually, there being a considerable drop from the balcony onto the rocky hillside below.

Not that she gazed down for more than a split second, her eyes soon returning to admire the view, which was as spectacular as Jack had promised.

In truth, Vivienne had never seen a view like it, not just for its natural beauty but for the sheer size and expanse of the panorama. It felt like she was standing on a mountaintop looking out over treetops at the bay beyond. She had no idea how large Port Stephens was but it looked enormous! And so beautiful and blue. Of course, it was a cloudless spring day, so the colour of the water reflected the blue of the sky. Perhaps on a rainy day it might not look so spectacular. But today, Mother Nature was on show and it took Vivienne's breath away.

Though not quite to the degree that Jack's holding her hand a minute ago had taken it away.

Vivienne still could not get over the intensity of her physical response to something as simple as hand-holding. Her mind boggled at what she might do if Jack ever kissed her, or touched her in a more intimate fashion.

Not that he was likely to, so she was safe on that score. But just thinking about it sent an erotically charged shiver trickling down her spine. Her hands tightened on the railing when Jack moved to stand beside her.

'Well?' he said somewhat smugly. 'It is an incredible view, isn't it?'

Vivienne gritted her teeth as she turned to face him. '"Incredible" hardly describes it, Jack,' she said, proud that she could sound so calm when she felt anything but. It was as well, however, that she was wearing sunglasses. They gave her a degree of safety. 'I guess, if I had the money, I'd be tempted to buy this place too. That is one seductive view.'

'It's even better from the top floor,' he said. 'Shall we go take a look?'

What could she say? *No, I don't think so, Jack. And no, I'm sorry, but I won't be taking this job after all.* He'd want to know why and she couldn't tell him the truth, could she? Couldn't confess suddenly to lusting after him with a lust to rival what Paris had felt for

Helen of Troy. He'd think she'd gone barmy! Which, of course, she had. Totally, tragically barmy!

'Shouldn't you show me the downstairs apartments first?' she said.

'That can wait. Come on.'

'You lead the way,' she said quickly before he could reach for her hand again. 'I'll be right behind you.'

Being behind Jack wasn't totally without trouble; Vivienne was having difficulty keeping her eyes off his very nice butt, especially once he started up the stairs. In desperation she dropped her gaze to her feet until she reached the upper level which opened out into a spacious semi-circular landing, over which hung a very elaborate crystal chandelier.

'I gather this was once Francesco's private art gallery,' Jack said. 'But, as you can see,' he went on, waving a hand towards where several paintings obviously had once hung against the heavily embossed wallpaper, 'All the pictures are now gone.'

'Would you like it to be an art gallery again?' Vivienne asked, doing her best to refocus on business.

Jack shrugged. 'I'll leave that decision up to you. I know I'll like whatever you do with it.'

Oh dear, Vivienne thought with some dismay, only too aware that she was slowly being sucked into a situation from which there was no escape. Because in truth she really wanted to do this job, wanted to transform Francesco's Folly into the type of home Jack would love. His faith in her abilities was extremely flattering. And the house itself was a fantastic challenge. It was impossible to say no. And yet she knew she should. Nothing good was going to come out of working side by side with Jack. She could feel it in her bones—and several other parts of her body as well!

'This way,' he said, and walked over to the double doors in the centre of the semi-circular wall, throwing them both open and waving her inside with a flourish of his right arm.

Vivienne walked past him into a massive rectangular-shaped living room, which she knew instantly would look fabulous if and when it was properly refurbished. Her designer's eyes were picturing the room with its hideous wallpaper stripped off, the walls painted white and the dated furniture replaced by more modern pieces. The marble fireplace at the far end of the room could stay, but the rest would have to go, especially the heavy brocade curtains which framed the glass doors leading out onto the balcony, and which were simply horrible.

'I can see that decorating head of yours is already ticking away, Vivienne,' Jack said, smiling as he headed over to the glass doors. 'But first things first, madam. The view!'

Even from where she was standing Vivienne could see that the view from up here was even more spectacular than from the lower balcony. But to get there she had to brush past Jack, who was still standing in the half-opened doorway, waiting for her. She somehow managed to move past him without actually making bodily contact, hurrying over to the railing like the hounds of hell were after her. But as she closed her fingers over the top rung, leaning her weight against it at the same time, the whole thing suddenly shifted.

CHAPTER NINE

JACK SAW THE railing give way a split second before Vivienne screamed. With a burst of fear-fuelled adrenaline, he covered the distance between them with a speed which would later amaze him, grabbing at Vivienne as she began to lose her balance, her arms flailing wildly, her sunglasses flying off her face into the valley below. All he got hold of at first was the back of her suit jacket but it was enough to stop the momentum of her fall. Finally he managed to wind one firm arm around her waist and pull her back from where she was still teetering on the edge of disaster. She fell back against him, her scream silenced as she gasped for air. By the time he dragged her body back further from the edge of the balcony, her shock had turned to an almost hysterical sobbing.

This time, Jack didn't hesitate to comfort her, turning her trembling body in his arms and holding her close.

'There there,' he murmured, one of his arms wrapped tightly around her lower back whilst the other gently stroked the nape of her neck. 'Stop crying. You're safe.'

But she didn't stop crying. She wept on and on, Jack suspecting that her close brush with death might have released more emotions than just relief. Possibly she was crying over what had been happening in her life recently.

Whatever, having her pressed hard against him was not conducive to his peace of mind. Or the peace of his body. Despite willing his sex-starved flesh to stay calm, it did not. Common sense demanded he push her away from him. But to do so whilst she was still sobbing so disconsolately seemed heartless. All he could hope for was that she wouldn't notice he was getting an erection.

Things went from bad to worse, however, when she moved her arms from where they'd been jammed between their chests and wound them tightly around his back, her head nestling into the crook of his neck. Now he could feel the soft fullness of her breasts, not to mention the warmth of her breath against his skin. When her crying finally stopped, he tried moving his lower half away from hers but it was almost impossible with the way she was clinging to him.

'Vivienne,' he said a bit brusquely.

Her head lifted, her tear-stained face no less beautiful, her lovely green eyes searching his with a strange intensity. And then she did something which shocked him. She planted her hands on his shoulders, reached up on tiptoe and kissed him full on the mouth. When he jerked his head backwards, her hands fell away and she sank back down on her heels, her face crumpling.

'I'm sorry,' she choked out. 'I thought…I thought… Oh, it doesn't matter what I thought. Obviously I was wrong.' And she staggered back from him, her shoulders slumping, her eyes wretchedly unhappy.

'No. You thought right, Vivienne. I've been struggling with my desire for you since I saw you naked in that bath yesterday. It's come as a surprise to me, I admit, but I want you, and I'd like to take you to bed more than anything. But not like this, Vivienne.'

She lifted startled eyes to his. 'What do you mean, not like this?'

Jack sighed as he pushed his sunglasses up on top of his head. 'Your kiss just now. It wasn't for me, not really. It was just a reaction to your close call with death. An instinctive wish to feel still alive.'

'No,' she denied quite fiercely. 'That isn't true. It *was* for you.'

Jack stared at her, shock rendering him speechless.

'I'm not sure I understand this sudden sexual attraction I have for you any more than you understand yours for me,' she swept on. 'Since we're being brutally honest here, till yesterday I never even *liked* you, let alone fancied you. It was weird, the way I started having these wicked thoughts about you.'

'What kind of wicked thoughts?' he asked her.

Vivienne shook her head. 'I…I've tried to work them out because they don't make sense. All I know is that I want you to make love to me. Very much so.'

Jack did his best to stay cool. Despite dying to put her words to the test, he suspected that if he wanted any kind of relationship with Vivienne—as opposed to just a quickie—then he needed to show some sensitivity to her present, highly vulnerable state. If he rushed her into bed right at this moment—there *was* a king-sized one in the nearby master bedroom, he recalled—she might regret it afterwards. At the same time, the temptation to do just that was almost irresistible.

'Hell, Vivienne, you shouldn't say things like that.'

'Why not? It's true. Crazy, perhaps, but true.'

He didn't like the 'crazy' bit.

'Kiss me, Jack,' she begged. *'Please.'*

Oh God, he thought as his groin twitched painfully. 'If I kiss you, I won't stop at kissing,' he told her bluntly.

She didn't say a word, just closed her eyes and parted her lips in the most provocative fashion.

Jack groaned, then pulled her back into his arms—hard—his head swooping down at the same time.

It was not a tender or loving kiss. It was rough and ravaging, his hands lifting to hold her face solidly captive so there was no escape from his merciless assault on her mouth.

Not that she tried to escape; Vivienne moaned her surrender the moment his lips crashed down on hers. Her body melted against his, the soft swell of her stomach pressing against his erection. This only inflamed Jack further, his teeth nipping and tugging at her lips until they felt swollen and hot. She gasped when he ran his tongue over their burning surfaces, moaning when at last his tongue darted deep into her mouth.

Jack's gut tightened when her lips closed tightly around him, sucking him in even deeper. He immediately started imagining what it would be like when she did that to other parts of his body. Which she would at some stage, he was sure. Although a cool character on the surface, Vivienne was obviously a wildly passionate woman underneath. A woman who liked sex and needed it. The perfect candidate to become his lover. Or even girlfriend, if that was what she wanted. He didn't much care, as long as he could have her in his bed on a regular basis.

When he tore his mouth away from hers, she moaned again, her green eyes glazed when they opened to stare dazedly up at him.

'Don't say a word,' he bit out. 'I'm not stopping altogether. Just till I get a couple of things straight.'

She didn't say a word. He suspected she was almost beyond talking, a fact he found rather flattering.

'I don't want this to be just a one-night stand,' he said. 'Or should I say, a one-day stand. I like you, Vivienne. Very much so. I want more from you than that. Tell me now if this idea doesn't appeal to you, then I won't start making plans for afterwards. If you say you don't like me enough to consider a relationship with me, then after this once, we'll have to go our separate ways. Because once we cross this line, sweetheart, there will be no working together unless we're sleeping together.'

Jack hoped Vivienne didn't see his ultimatum as a form of sexual harassment, or even blackmail. He was just telling her as it was. He wasn't her boss. Yet. But by God he wanted to be, especially in the bedroom.

Hot images danced in his head of her obeying his every command and demand; of her going down on him wherever and whenever he wanted; of her being tied naked to various pieces of furniture, totally at his mercy. All silly fantasies, he suspected. Because, as passionate as Vivienne seemed to be, she wasn't the submissive type. Though who knew? Maybe she would enjoy being dominated in the bedroom.

His earlier fierce arousal, which had subsided somewhat with his talking, came back with a vengeance.

'You don't need to give me your answer right now,' he ground out to a still silent but flushed Vivienne. 'Afterwards will do.' Unable to wait another second, Jack swept her up into his arms and headed for the master bedroom. When his sunglasses fell off the back of his head in the process, he didn't bother to stop and pick them up.

CHAPTER TEN

VIVIENNE'S HEAD WHIRLED with conflicting thoughts as she clamped her hands around Jack's neck and burrowed her face into the base of his throat. What remained of her sense of decency demanded that she stop him right now. She liked Jack somewhat better than she had, but to have sex with him wasn't right—surely?

But the voice of decency wasn't nearly as powerful as the voice of desire. It obliterated and overwhelmed all objections with its promise of excitement and pleasure. Jack's impassioned kiss had given her a taste of what was to come. Not just excitement and pleasure, but abandonment and satisfaction. The kind of abandonment which she'd always secretly craved. The kind of satisfaction which she'd never really enjoyed.

Somehow, Vivienne knew that in Jack's arms she would become a different woman from the one who'd kept her virginity until she was twenty-one, and who'd remained a shy, timid lover in the years since that first, uninspiring initiation into sex. With Jack, she would be wild and wanton. Maybe even wicked. Already her lips were opening to kiss his neck. Though it wasn't a kiss for long, more of a slow, sensual sucking at his skin, her heartbeat quickening at the sheer audacity of her action.

When he groaned and tipped his head to one side,

her mouth clamped him more tightly, as if she were some rabid vampire.

This time he wrenched his head away before setting her down abruptly in the middle of a large room, which was devoid of all furniture except for a huge bed, which looked new, its striped red-and-white bedding totally at odds with the pale blue shag-pile carpet and faded floral wallpaper. The air in the room was a little musty but surprisingly warm, probably because the sliding glass doors which led out onto the east-facing balcony would have caught the morning sun. Jack left her to go over and open one of those doors before turning and shaking his head at her.

'Do you have any idea what kind of teasing I'll get at work with a love bite on my neck?' he said, and rubbed at the spot on his neck that she'd been ravaging.

Vivienne tried to summon up some shame but it seemed she was beyond it. 'I can't imagine any of your employees daring to tease you.'

Jack chuckled. 'In that case, you don't know men very well.'

'Perhaps not,' she murmured, the thought occurring to her that she didn't know herself very well either. Certainly not this new uninhibited self, the one who was much more daring—and a lot more exciting—than the Vivienne she was used to.

'Not to worry,' Jack said and took off his jacket, tossing it onto the carpet with typical male nonchalance. 'I'll wear a shirt with a collar for a few days. But please,' he added as he stripped off his T-shirt, 'try to confine that sexy mouth of yours to areas of mine normally covered by clothes.'

'Yes, boss,' she said as she ogled his quite magnificent male body. His shoulders were impressively broad, his arms bulging with muscles, his chest superbly sculptured and nicely tanned with surprisingly little body hair, just a smattering of curls in the centre, plus a narrow line of them arrowing down past his six-pack, ending at his navel. His hips were slender but his thighs looked massive in those tight jeans.

So did something else…

Vivienne had always thought she would never be attracted to a big man; that their sheer size would intimidate her.

Well, guess what, Vivienne? You were dead wrong!

Her breath caught when he snapped open the waistband on his jeans, her heartbeat suspending as he ran the zip down.

'Why aren't you getting undressed?' he threw over at her as he peeled off his jeans, revealing a huge bulge in his black underpants. 'Don't tell me you've gone all shy on me. Come now, Vivienne, you and I both know that the uptight image you project at work is not the real you at all. You're hot stuff, sweetheart.'

Vivienne certainly felt hot at that moment. Her face flamed as she gulped then sucked in a much-needed breath.

Jack smiled a decidedly smug smile. 'Ah, I get it. You like to watch. Fine by me,' he said, and took off his remaining underwear.

Oh my… And she'd thought Daryl was reasonably well-equipped.

Compared to Jack, Daryl was… Well, he just didn't compare! No wonder Jack wasn't shy about showing off his body; he was incredible, Vivienne thought as her admiring gaze ran over him once again from top to toe.

'You *do* like to watch, don't you?' he said as he reached for his discarded jeans and extracted his wallet from the back pocket. 'Can't say I'm much of a watcher. But with you, lovely Vivienne, I'm going to make an exception.'

Vivienne was taken aback when, after taking a condom out of his wallet and tossing the wallet back down on his jeans, Jack walked over to the bed. He stretched out on top of the duvet, dropping the small foil packet he was holding onto his chest before looping his hands behind his head and acting for all the world like he wasn't stark naked with an erection the size of the Eiffel Tower.

'Okay,' he said, 'I'm ready to watch. Take your clothes off. But very slowly, please. I want to savour every moment.'

When she just stood there, dry-mouthed and motionless, he shot her an intense look. 'Come now, Vivienne, what are you waiting for? You know patience is not one of my virtues.'

When she hesitated further, her new, wicked self started whispering in her ear.

Yes, Vivienne, what are you waiting for? You want to take your clothes off for him. You know you do. You want to see him look at your breasts the way he did yesterday. You want to see those hard blue eyes glitter with lust for you. More than anything, you want to abandon every inferior feeling you've ever had about yourself when to comes to sex. Jack thinks you're hot stuff. Then be hot stuff, girl. It's now or never!

Her hands still shook as she took off her jacket slowly—very slowly—the way Jack had ordered. She hated the thought of dropping it on the floor, such an action going against Vivienne's compulsion to keep everything neat and tidy. But, since there weren't any chairs in the room, she really had no option. In a weird kind of way, actually letting the jacket drop from her fingers onto the carpet produced a strangely liberating buzz. By the time her hands went to the top button of her shirt, Vivienne was surprised to see that they were no longer shaking. Her breathing had quickened, however. Not from nerves; from excitement. She watched Jack's eyes as she flicked open each button. They weren't on her face, of course. They were riveted to her chest.

It did bother Vivienne slightly that she was wearing a white cotton minimiser bra rather than the kind of lacy half-cup push-up number Jack was probably expecting. After all, he'd made it clear he believed that underneath her cool, career-woman surface she was a seriously sexy babe, the sort of woman who would wear seriously sexy underwear.

As much as she liked that idea, Jack was, unfortunately, mistaken. All she could hope for was that he wouldn't care once she took the darned thing off. He'd obviously liked the look of her breasts yesterday so she wasn't shy about showing them off to him. Frankly, she no longer felt at all shy. Amazing!

His eyes remained glued to her chest whilst she peeled her blouse back off her shoulders and let it flutter down to the floor. His expression didn't change at the sight of her cotton bra, though Vivienne was quick to remove the less-than-flattering garment from her body. Now his eyes narrowed, his lips parting slightly as he drew in a ragged breath then let it out slowly. Finally, his eyes lifted to her face.

'Has anyone ever told you that you have the most beautiful breasts in the world?'

'No,' she replied truthfully. Daryl had said how beautiful she was all the time, but he'd never singled out her breasts for his compliments.

'I find that hard to believe. They are incredible. I

could look at them all day. But I'd infinitely prefer to touch them.' he said as he removed his hands from behind his head.

Vivienne's nipples responded to his declaration of intent by standing to attention in the most flagrant fashion. Obviously they wanted to be touched as much as Jack wanted to touch them. She removed the rest of her clothes in one brisk movement, thereby hiding her rather unflattering white cotton briefs. On top of that, it didn't allow time for her mind to fill with negative thoughts about her wide hips or soft stomach, or the many other physical flaws which worried her from time to time. Jack might think her breasts perfect but not all men liked full breasts, or hourglass figures.

Her first serious boyfriend—the insensitive creep— had told her that he actually preferred skinny girls. But he'd *loved* that she was a virgin. Needless to say, their relationship hadn't lasted, and Vivienne had taken some considerable time before she'd risked her heart—and her body—a second time.

Fortunately, she didn't have to worry about her heart this time, since she wasn't in love with Jack.

'You are one seriously beautiful woman,' he said thickly, his hot gaze reflecting his admiration. 'Now get yourself over here, Vivienne. I've done enough watching for one day.'

Never in her life had Vivienne felt as sexy—or as excited—as she did at that moment.

'Coming, boss,' she said in a low, sultry voice, sashaying over to stand at the side of the bed.

Jack looked her slowly up and down with a decidedly lascivious gaze. 'Mmm. I like it when you call me that.'

For some weird and wonderful reason, she liked calling him that too. Strange, when normally she found his bossy ways extremely irritating.

'Okay, Vivienne,' he went on. 'Take this condom here and put it on me. I don't think I can manage after that wicked striptease of yours.'

Vivienne wasn't sure that she could manage, either. She'd never put a condom on before. But no way was she going to tell him that. Any self-respecting sexually experienced woman should be able to slip on protection with their eyes closed. 'Truly,' she said with just the right amount of droll exasperation as she picked up the foil packet and ripped it open the way she'd seen Daryl do. 'Are you sure this will fit?' She stared down at the small circle of rubber.

Jack sighed. 'Here. Give it to me.'

She happily handed it over. 'Yes, boss.'

'Truly,' he said, copying her earlier droll tone to a tee.

When she laughed, he did too.Their eyes met, her heart squeezing tight as her stomach flipped over. The old Vivienne might have imagined there was more going on between them than just sex. The new Vivienne knew exactly what was causing her physical responses. Her eyes dropped to where Jack was expertly rolling the condom over the full length of his amazing erection, her mouth drying as she tried to imagine how it would feel inside her.

'I hope you like being on top,' Jack said once protection was completed. 'I don't usually like to hand over control, but I don't dare touch you at the moment. You've driven me to the brink. So help me out here. I'm feeling decidedly fragile.'

Vivienne gnawed at her bottom lip. What to say? If she confessed she didn't care for that position, he would think she was lying. Vivienne swallowed, telling herself firmly that she could do this. It wasn't rocket science. And she *had* done it before. Briefly. A couple of times. *Just climb up onto the bed. Now throw one leg over him. Don't think about what he can see. Just kneel up over him. Yes, that's the way. Now take him in your right hand.* Heavens, he *was* big. *What if he doesn't fit in you?*

But he did—deliciously so—sliding into her with shocking ease, Vivienne holding her breath as she lowered herself slowly down till she was sitting on him, his swollen sex filling her in a way she'd never felt filled before. She closed her eyes so that she could savour the blissful sensation, breathing out whilst rocking back and forth at the same time.

His groan startled her, her eyes flying open. He was lying there looking tortured, his breathing ragged, his hands curled into white-knuckled fists by his side.

'Stop moving like that, for pity's sake,' he ground out.

Vivienne was shocked at how much she liked his being close to losing control.

'But I want to move,' she purred, and did so, rising and falling upon him with a slow, sensual rhythm.

He didn't groan this time. He swore, then reached for her, grabbing her shoulders and throwing her roughly round and under him. Now she *couldn't* move, his hands and his weight pinning her to the bed.

'I should have known you wouldn't do as you were told for too long,' he growled. 'You're too strong willed.' He smiled a devilishly sexy smile.

Vivienne couldn't believe it when her own lips curved upwards in a saucy smile of her own. 'Maybe I prefer it this way.'

'Mmm. Now *that* I don't believe. Women of your obvious experience *never* prefer the missionary position.'

Vivienne tried not to laugh. But it was rather funny, given the limited range of her sexual experience.

'Do you always talk this much when having sex?' she asked him.

'Only when I need to get my act together. I've never been fond of ending a good thing too soon. It would be especially disappointing on this occasion, when I might be relegated to one time only.'

'Oh, I don't think that's very likely, Jack,' she said, green eyes glittering up at his. 'I can't imagine not wanting at least seconds from a man of your rather... obvious attractions.' Lord, but was it really her saying that? Talk about wicked!

'Well, that's good to know, Vivienne. But, just in case you change your mind afterwards, we're going to do this the way *I* prefer.'

Vivienne gasped when he abruptly withdrew, her mind spinning when he turned her over, wrapping one of his huge arms around her waist as he scooped her up on all fours.

Dear heaven, she thought dazedly.

As personally inexperienced as Vivienne was in the many sexual positions possible, she wasn't ignorant. She knew exactly what Jack was going to do. She could feel him right behind her but she couldn't see him, her wide eyes seeing nothing but the wallpapered wall above the bed. There was no question of resisting him, not once he re-entered her, and certainly not once he took hold of her breasts and started moving inside her. Immediately, any rational thinking shut down, her desire-laden brain making all her decisions for her, demanding that she move with him, her hips rocking back and forth in a frantic rhythm, her body searching for release from the almost torturous tension building up inside her.

Vivienne had never understood the concept of pain being closely linked with pleasure. But she understood now, even more so when Jack started squeezing her already burning nipples. Just when Vivienne thought she could not bear the sensations any longer, Jack removed his hands and pressed her upper body down onto the bed, the position emphasising her raised hips and bottom, her face flaming with a heady combination of embarrassment and excitement. When he stopped moving, she moaned in frustration, her buttocks clenching tightly together as he caressed them with long, slow, circular strokes of his very big hands.

'Do you like this?' he said thickly as his hands caressed her sensitive flesh. She tried to feel shocked but all she felt was a dark, delicious pleasure.

'Yes,' she choked out.

'Another time, then,' he said, and took hold of her hips once more. This time he thrust faster and deeper, Vivienne struggling to stay silent the way she usually did during sex. She tried muffling her moans in a nearby pillow, but in the end she could not contain the animal sounds which escaped her lips. Her moans became groans, her fingers scrunching up great handfuls of duvet as her whole body spun out of control.

She came with a rush, her release as fast as a balloon bursting. One moment she was suspended in a type of erotic agony, the next all that dreadful tension was gone, replaced by great waves of pleasure washing through her, pulling her one way then another, like the tide. She bit her lip to stop herself from crying out. Jack didn't bother with such niceties, roaring out his satisfaction as he held her tight and shuddered into her for an incredibly long time.

By the time he finally finished, Vivienne's own incredible orgasm had just faded away, her limbs succumbing to a languor which would have seen her flopping face down on the bed if Jack hadn't been holding her up.

Slowly, and with surprising gentleness, he withdrew then lowered her onto the bed where she closed her eyes and sighed the type of sigh she'd never sighed before. It contained nothing but total sexual satisfaction.

'Don't go away now,' he murmured, and dropped a kiss in the small of her back.

She would have laughed if she'd had the energy.

Vivienne vaguely heard the sound of a toilet flushing and water running. Was he having a shower? she wondered.

It was her last thought before sleep claimed her.

CHAPTER ELEVEN

JACK DIDN'T REALISE Vivienne was sound asleep until he came back from the bathroom. She didn't reply to his telling her he was going to go down the road to buy some supplies, and was there anything particular she would like to eat.

Poor darling, he thought as he looked down at her luscious but unconscious form. She was obviously exhausted, not just from the sex but from everything else she'd endured lately. Best let her sleep, at least for a while.

Very quietly Jack put on his clothes and left the room, making his way to the nearby kitchen, where he rifled through the various cupboards and drawers till he found paper and a pen. Writing Vivienne an explanatory note, he returned to the bedroom where he propped the note against her pile of clothes, careful not to look at her lest he be overcome with desire for her once more. Time enough for those seconds she'd mentioned after they'd both had some lunch.

Not that he had any intention of stopping at mere seconds. Or of letting Vivienne say no to becoming his lover on a more regular basis. Anyone could see what Vivienne needed at this point in her life. Besides, being kept busy with work, she needed a man who would make mad, passionate love to her as often as possible; who would make her see that her life wasn't over just because she'd been dumped by some fortune-hunting bastard.

Jack believed he was that man.

He'd even offer his friendship, if she wanted it.

Jack frowned at this last thought, recalling how Vivienne had said earlier that she'd never liked him all that much. He wondered why that was. Still, that had been *before* she'd got to know him. And he wasn't just referring to their getting to know each other in the biblical sense. They'd actually talked to each other more in the last two days than in all the years Vivienne had worked for him. He'd certainly confided more to her than he had to any other woman. He'd even told her about his mother's lover! Jack liked it that Vivienne hadn't been judgemental about anything, especially his decision not to marry and have children, saying he had the right to live his life as he saw fit.

She was like him, in a way, practical and pragmatic, with a sensible head on her shoulders. Except when it came to that Daryl creep. Of course, dear old Daryl had obviously been clever, saying and doing all the right things to get Vivienne hooked. No doubt he'd thought he was on to a good wicket, until a better one had come along. Or so he'd mistakenly imagined. The fool had no idea what he was getting into, marrying Courtney Ellison. Still, they were a well-matched pair, both totally without morals or consciences. Vivienne didn't realise how lucky she was, not to have married a man like that.

Jack was about to leave the room when there was a sound from the bed. For a split second, he thought Vivienne had woken up. But she hadn't. She'd just rolled over and curled herself up in the foetal position, moving her peach-like bottom into a highly provocative curve. Jack suppressed a groan, then very carefully lifted up the end of the duvet and placed it over her. Unfortunately, it only went as far as her waist, leaving her upper half on show.

As he stared down at her, Jack's mind went back to that moment when he'd taken her on all fours, her lush breasts cradled in his hands. He recalled how she'd moaned when he'd squeezed her nipples; how she'd rocked back and forth on her knees, slapping her buttocks against his hip; how she'd cried out when she finally came. Jack couldn't remember being with a woman who'd come as hard as she had. It had felt incredible, being inside her at that moment.

'Better not think about that right now,' he muttered to himself and hurried downstairs, locking the front doors behind him before climbing into his car and driving off. Time enough for such thoughts after he'd had lunch; his stomach was telling him it was eating time. Jack remembered passing a small shopping centre on the way here where they were sure to have everything he would need for the rest of day.

Vivienne woke to the sound of silence, plus the realisation that at some stage Jack had covered her with the bottom half of the duvet. Sitting up, she glanced around the empty room, looking and listening for evidence of where he might have gone to. There were no sounds coming from anywhere nearby, other than some distant chirping of birds. Surely Jack wouldn't have left her alone in the house? Alone and naked.

A shiver ran down her spine.

It was then that she saw the note. Swinging her feet over the side of the bed, Vivienne reached down to pick it up, sighing with relief as she read his message. Not that she seriously imagined Jack would run out on her. Why would he, when he no doubt thought he'd now solved two problems with one Vivienne? His need for an interior designer, plus his need for a sexual partner. After the act she'd just put on for him in bed, he would naturally conclude she would agree to whatever he wanted.

But it hadn't been an act, had it? Vivienne accepted with a degree of confusion. She'd been genuinely swept away with desire and passion for the man. She'd enjoyed everything they'd done together, thrilling to her new, uninhibited self. As for that mind-blowing orgasm… A girl would have to be insane not to want more of those.

Why was it, Vivienne puzzled, that she'd never experienced anything like that with Daryl? After all, she'd been madly in love with the man. But not once had she been carried away in bed the way she had been with Jack. Not once had she come with *Daryl* inside her. Surely it couldn't just be a question of size? She didn't believe that. After all, she'd been panting for Jack before he'd taken off his clothes. She'd been panting for him back in the restaurant yesterday, for pity's sake!

It was all very perplexing.

The sound of a car roaring up the steep driveway sent Vivienne into a momentary panic. As wildly uninhibited as she'd been during sex with Jack, no way did she want him walking in on her still in the nude.

Scooping up her clothes, she raced over to the door which she presumed led into a bathroom. And, yes, it *was* a bathroom…in a fashion.

'Oh, lordie, lordie, lordie!' she exclaimed, laughing.

Vivienne did know that, in theory, pink and black bathrooms had been all the rage at some stage last century but she'd never actually seen one. Talk about hideous! Shaking her head in wry amusement, she closed the door behind her. After using the black toilet and washing her hands in the pink vanity basin, she quickly dressed. She was finger-combing her hair in the large but chipped wall mirror when there was a sharp rapping on the bathroom door.

'You in there, Vivienne?' Jack called out.

'Er…yes; I'm getting dressed,' she said, feeling suddenly awkward with him, not to mention embarrassed. It seemed the old Vivienne was rearing her uptight head once again.

'I've bought us some food,' Jack said as he opened the door and walked straight in.

'Don't you believe in knocking?' she said sharply.

He looked taken aback. 'I thought I did.'

'Well, yes, but you should still wait till I invite you to enter.'

'Mmm. Your mood seems to have deteriorated since I left. I dare say you're mad at me for not staying to give you those seconds you wanted. Sorry, beautiful, but aside from the condom issue I'm afraid men of my size need constant refuelling.'

Vivienne wished he hadn't mentioned his size. Or her rather brazen statement about having seconds. The wanton hussy who'd said those things suddenly seemed to have disappeared, which bothered her. Because she liked that hussy. She liked her a lot. All Vivienne could hope was that once Jack started making love to her again—which he would, sooner or later—she'd turn back into that exciting new Vivienne again.

Not that she'd entirely reverted to the old Vivienne, the one who'd been taken in by the likes of Daryl. That seriously pathetic creature was gone for good!

'So, what do you think of the bathroom?' Jack went on.

'What? Oh yes, the bathroom. It's seriously awful.'

Jack chuckled. 'Wait till you see the others. The worst is all brown with a yucky olive-green spa bath in the corner.'

'Good Lord.'

'The kitchens are slightly better, as long as you like pine. Speaking of kitchens, that's where I left the food. I'm afraid it's just hamburgers, fries and Coke—but I figured, who doesn't like hamburgers, fries and Coke?'

Once again, he didn't wait for her to reply, just took her hand and led her from the bathroom, out through the bedroom and down a short hallway into a large country-style kitchen where, yes, pine was the order of the day. There were pine cupboards as well as pine benchtops, and three pine stools lined up at the pine breakfast bar. Not that it mattered. Vivienne felt pretty sure that Jack would want the whole interior of this house stripped bare and totally redone.

'Have a seat,' Jack said, pulling out a pine stool for her before picking up one of the others and carrying it round to the other side.

When she frowned at his action, he smiled over at her. 'Have to keep my distance till I've eaten,' he said. 'I can't think about sex and eat at the same time, and every time I get close to you, beautiful, I think about sex.'

Vivienne could not help feeling flattered by his remark, though his calling her beautiful all the time was beginning to grate. 'I find that hard to believe,' she said somewhat tartly.

His smile widened. 'Come now, Vivienne, you don't fool me for a minute with that act of yours. Now, eat up and stop pretending you don't want to get back to bed as quickly as I do.'

Vivienne opened her mouth to say something more, then closed it again. Because Jack was right. There was no point in denying it. No point in saying anything at all! So she reached for the food and started eating.

Neither of them spoke as they each consumed their hamburger, which was more delicious than any hamburger Vivienne had ever eaten—king-sized and truly mouthwatering, with the kind of ingredients you only got at a small café. The fries weren't half bad, either— golden and crispy with just the right amount of salt. As for the Coke… Vivienne sighed with pleasure as she washed the meal down with her favourite drink. The only fault she could find was that Jack hadn't bought Diet Coke, opting instead for the full-strength variety.

'Do you realise how much sugar is contained in this one small bottle?' Vivienne said after downing all of it.

'Not enough to send a rocket to the moon,' Jack replied. 'But enough to spark lift-off in yours truly,' he added with the wickedest smile, his blue eyes glittering with sexual intent at the same time.

Vivienne struggled to act cool under an immediate quickening of her heart. Although she wasn't about to play hard to get—it was a little late for that—she didn't want to appear too easy. Or too eager.

'I thought you'd give me the grand tour of the house first,' she said, casually picking up one of the paper serviettes which came with the meal and dabbing at the corners of her mouth.

'Then you thought wrong,' he said.

Vivienne glowered at him. This was why she'd never liked working for Jack. He was far too bossy. It was always his way or the highway. She used to have to put up with it when she was an employee of Classic Design. But she didn't have to put up with it now.

'Don't I have any say in the matter?' she asked with a toss of her head.

He looked taken aback for a second. But then he smiled. 'Of course you do. Far be it from me to force you to do anything you didn't want to do. I have too much respect for you for that. So which would you rather do, Vivienne? Look around this house for a dreary hour or so, or go have some more fantastic fun in bed?'

Vivienne sighed. 'You are a clever, conniving devil, do you know that?'

He grinned. 'I'll take that as a compliment.'

'Then you'd be wrong!'

'You mean you're opting for the grand tour?'

She shook her head at him. 'You know I'm not. But that doesn't mean I'll always do whatever you want.'

'Are you sure about that?'

She wasn't. But no way was she going to admit it. 'The trouble with you, Jack Stone, is you are way too used to getting your own way.'

'I have to confess I like being the boss, especially in the bedroom.'

'I gathered that already.'

'And I gathered you liked it that way.'

Vivienne rolled her eyes. He really was terribly arrogant. And super-confident when it came to sex. She wondered if that was due to his impressive equipment, or wealth of experience. Whatever the reason, Vivienne had no intention of letting him run this show entirely.

'As a modern woman living in the twenty-first century,' she said coolly, 'I expect that any sexual relationship we have will be conducted as equals.'

'Fair enough,' he said.

'There will be rules involved,' Vivienne stated firmly.

His eyebrows arched. 'What kind of rules?'

Vivienne had absolutely no idea. It was time to im-prove. And quickly. 'Firstly, you will always use a condom.' No way was she going to tell him she was on the pill.

'You won't have any argument with me on that score,' Jack said. 'That's why I went out and bought a dozen.'

'A dozen!' she exclaimed, stunned at the thought he might use so many during one short afternoon.

Jack shrugged. 'Better to be safe than sorry. Besides, what we don't use today will keep till tomorrow.'

Vivienne blinked. 'What do you mean, tomorrow? Surely you have work to do tomorrow? I know you, Jack. You're a workaholic.'

'True. But there's always after work. I thought I'd take you out somewhere swanky in the city for dinner, then back to my place for afters,' he added somewhat salaciously.

'You really are incorrigible,' Vivienne scolded, de-spite secretly looking forward to being his afters tomor-row night. 'Rule number two is that you *ask* me, Jack, not just tell me.'

'Oh. Right. Okay, would you like to go out to din-ner tomorrow night?'

'Maybe. I'll give you my answer later.'

'Nope. That won't do, Vivienne. I have some rules of my own—the main one being, if and when I ask you something, I get a straight answer. Because I'm a straight kind of guy. I won't play word games. So is it a yes or a no?'

Vivienne rather liked it that he wouldn't let her muck him around. At the same time, she wasn't about to say yes every time. 'It's a yes to dinner. You'll have to ask me again tomorrow night about afters. I'm not sure how

I'll feel about more sex so soon after today.' And what a load of crock that was!

He looked hard at her, and then he smiled. 'Fair enough. Any more rules?'

'I...I...can't think of any more right now. But I reserve the right to add to the list if something important occurs to me.'

'Same here,' Jack said as he reached into the plastic bag which lay next to him and retrieved the box of condoms he'd told her about. 'Okay, now that I know your rules and we've finished eating, I'll ask you again. Very politely. Do you want a grand tour of the house first, or more sex?'

Vivienne swallowed. She knew what she wanted to say but simply could not bring herself to say it.

Jack rose from the stool, ripping the cellophane off the box of condoms as he walked around to her. 'Of course, there is a third alternative,' he said, his eyes holding hers. 'We could combine the two.'

Vivienne just stared up at him, her tongue no longer working.

He reached out to run a tantalising finger around her slightly parted lips. Vivienne gasped when he sent that finger into her mouth, her head spinning, as suddenly she was that new Vivienne again, with all her wild, wanton boldness. Her lips closed around his finger, her green eyes glittering as she began a slow, sensual sucking.

'I take it that's a yes,' he said thickly.

CHAPTER TWELVE

'What do you think you're doing?' Vivienne said sharply when Jack picked up her camera and pointed it in her direction. Vivienne was lying back on one of the desk chairs, dressed in nothing but her white blouse, looking sinfully sexy with only one button done up.

'I'm taking a photograph of my beautiful new girl-friend?' he said.

'But I'm half-naked,' she protested, sitting up and pushing her hair back from her face. 'And...and my hair is messy.'

He laughed. 'Don't be silly. You look gorgeous.'

'I'm serious, Jack. I don't want you taking any photos of me like this. And I'm not your new girlfriend. Not really. We're lovers, that's all.'

Jack tried not to scowl. He should have been pleased that Vivienne wanted to restrict their relationship to a strictly sexual one. It was exactly what he'd thought he wanted. But after spending the whole day with her, he realised he wanted more from her than that.

'I wouldn't have asked you out to dinner tomorrow night if I wanted us to just be lovers,' he insisted. 'I like being with you, Vivienne. And talking to you. And not just about work-related matters. I want to spend time with you out of bed as well as in it. I would have thought that was obvious by now.' They hadn't spent the entire afternoon having sex. Between times they'd discussed the refurbishment of the house, whilst Vivienne had retrieved her camera from the car and taken photos of everything.

'I like spending time with you too,' she said. 'But—'

'So what's the problem?' he broke in, and put the camera down. 'Too soon after Daryl, is that it?'

Vivienne stared up at him. To be brutally honest she hadn't given Daryl a thought all afternoon. But now that Jack had brought him up, Vivienne wondered again if Daryl's dumping her so cruelly was the reason behind her amazing change of character. Maybe her turning into Vivienne the Vamp was really just a revenge thing. Or a rebound thing. Or something equally self-destructive.

Common sense demanded she step back from this whole situation for a while until she could think more clearly. All that great sex today seemed to have addled her brain, because agreeing to become Jack's girlfriend at this stage could be a foolish move. Rather like jumping from the frying pan into the fire.

Yet, despite all that common sense reasoning, she still *wanted* to agree. Quite desperately. It was one thing to say no to his taking candid photographs of her; she'd always hated having her photograph taken. It was quite another thing to say no to more sex with him. Which was what would happen if she refused to become his girlfriend. Jack was not the kind of man who warmed to rejection. He'd probably take back his offer of this job as well.

Of course, she could always make an alternative suggestion…

The idea which popped into her head was truly

wicked. But oh so tempting, her heart quickening as the audacious counter-proposal formed in her brain. Hopefully, Jack would agree. Oh, surely he would. He was a man, after all. And what she would be proposing was every man's fantasy.

Her mouth still dried with what she was about to suggest.

'For pity's sake say something, Vivienne,' Jack finally snapped. 'You must know how much I detest indecision.'

'I do too,' she threw back at him. 'So, yes, it's way too soon for me to consider being any man's girlfriend.' *Especially one who's already admitted to being emotionally bankrupt,* she thought, but didn't say. 'I'm not even keen on thinking of us as lovers. You and I both know that love has little to do with what we've been doing today. I'm not in love with you any more than you are with me. But there's no denying I love having sex with you. More than I would ever have thought possible.'

Vivienne could not help but notice this last statement of hers didn't go down too well. But Jack had claimed he liked honesty and she was only being honest.

'I dare say you might be shocked by what I am about to suggest…'

'I doubt anything you say now is going to shock me, Vivienne,' he said very drily. 'So suggest away.'

Vivienne buttoned up her blouse then took a deep breath before going on. 'Firstly let me say I would very much like to do this job,' she began, waving her hand up at the façade of Francesco's Folly. 'But, as you yourself said, it would be impossible for us to work together now without sleeping together. So, for the duration of this project, I would like to become your mistress.'

His head snapped back, his eyebrows arching at the same time. 'I guess I was wrong. You *have* shocked me. So, exactly what kind of mistress did you have in mind? The kind who dresses in shiny black leather and carries a whip?'

'Don't be silly,' she retorted.

'In that case, you must mean the kind I install in a flash apartment with all the bills paid, in exchange for which I get to do whatever I like to you whenever I like to do it.'

'I'm not that kind of girl, either.'

'That's a relief,' Jack said.

'I just meant the kind of mistress who's kept a secret. I don't want anyone and everyone knowing that we're sleeping together.'

'Why not? It wouldn't bother me if people knew.'

'Well, it would bother me.'

'Why?'

'Because it would lead to questions from friends and family that I don't want to answer.' Not that she had much of either. But Jack did.

'You're worried they might think badly of you,' he said. Quite intuitively, Vivienne thought.

She stood up. 'Yes, of course,' she said. Aside from how soon it was after Daryl, everyone she knew thought she didn't like Jack. They'd wonder what had come over her. They'd probably think she'd lost it.

Jack frowned. 'You wouldn't have to worry about that if you became my girlfriend.'

'But I don't *want* to become your girlfriend, Jack,' she said, feeling both irritated and frustrated with him. 'I just want to have sex with you, okay?'

Once again Jack looked none too pleased with her. 'Okay,' he bit out. 'Where?'

'What do you mean, *where*?'

'Just exactly that. Where are we going to do it? Not your place, I gather—or your good friend and neighbour Marion would twig, and then you'd have to answer those questions you don't want to answer. So that leaves my place, or a hotel room.'

Jack was taken aback when Vivienne blushed. Lord, but she was full of contradictions. In truth, he didn't know what to make of her today. Same as himself; why wasn't he happy with her mistress idea? Why was he trying to needle her? Nothing made sense to him any more. No, he knew *exactly* what was bugging him: his ego had been dented. His considerable ego.

Get a grip, Jack, he lectured himself sternly. *You're onto a good wicket here. If you don't stuff it up, that is. Think of the positives: all the sex you want with none of the complications. No clinging. No commitment. No having to say you love her. Exactly what the doctor ordered. So put aside your emotions and take a more pragmatic approach to Vivienne's offer which, if you think about it sensibly, was really rather exciting.*

'Obviously that idea doesn't appeal,' he said, trying hard not to sound sarcastic. 'Maybe you should rethink the idea about my getting you that flash apartment. I can afford it and it would solve the "where?" problem.'

As much as Vivienne was tempted to say yes—it *would* solve the 'where?' problem—she could see that such an arrangement went against her highly independent nature. Not to mention her conscience. She didn't want to feel Jack was *paying* her to have sex with him.

'Like I said, Jack, I'm not that sort of girl. Look, I have an alternative suggestion which I think would work well for both of us.'

Jack smothered the sigh which threatened to escape his lungs.

'Okay,' he said. 'Fire away.'

CHAPTER THIRTEEN

'THAT'S THE BEST news you could have told me,' Marion said.

They were sitting having morning tea in Vivienne's kitchen, Marion having dropped in to see how things had gone with Jack the previous day. Naturally Vivienne hadn't told Marion the whole rather shocking truth, just that she had accepted Jack's offer to redesign the interior of Francesco's Folly, as well as her plan to live at the place whilst the job was being done. Though that wouldn't be happening until contracts were exchanged in a couple of weeks.

Jack had seemed somewhat at odds with her live-in idea at first, until she'd pointed out that he could come visit her there every weekend, leaving him free during the week to concentrate on work. She'd boldly stated that she would be worth the wait, promising to be at his sexual beck and call for those two days. By the time Jack had dropped her back at her place late last night, he'd warmed to the idea, especially after having tested out what she meant by being at his sexual beck and call...

Vivienne, by then on the other hand, had been bombarded by a host of second thoughts. But she didn't voice them out loud, her sated body not having had second thoughts at all. She'd slept like a log last night and had woken feeling marvellous, any lingering qualms easily pushed aside.

Already she was looking forward to seeing Jack again tonight. He'd promised to take her somewhere discreet, although he'd argued that their having dinner together could easily be explained away as a business dinner. She was, after all, going to be working for him.

And under him. And on top of him, he'd added wickedly.

Vivienne struggled to contain the heat which flooded her veins at the memory of all Jack had demanded of her yesterday. Positions which she supposed weren't all that shocking, but which she'd never experienced before, let alone enjoyed. She was well aware of the woman being on top, but had never thought of it being done with the woman's back to her lover. But, oh…she'd loved it that way. Loved riding him with her hands clasped around the rungs of the brass bed-end. Loved it that she could not see him watching her. That way, she'd been able to lose herself in her pleasure, uncaring of anything but the gathering of tension deep within her body. Had she screamed out loud when she'd come? Yes. Yes, she had. She was sure she had.

Oh God.

Vivienne swallowed.

'Now I can go away next week without worrying about you,' Marion was saying.

Vivienne blinked. 'What was that? You're going away?' she asked a bit blankly.

Marion shook her head at her. 'I thought you might have forgotten, what with everything that's happened. I'm going to Europe for a holiday, remember? London first to visit some of my long-lost rellies, then over to

Paris, and then I'm going for a cruise down the Rhine. Be gone nearly six weeks. You've no idea how much I'm looking forward to it. It's been a long time since I had a decent holiday like that. But none of that for now. Tell me more about this house Jack bought. What's its name again?'

'Francesco's Folly.'

'Sounds rather romantic.'

Vivienne laughed. 'It's nothing of the kind,' she said, thinking that she would never associate that house with romance. Just sex, along with lust and uncontrollable passion.

Vivienne suddenly frowned. How odd. They were not words which she'd ever associated with herself. She'd never fallen in lust before or suffered from un-controllable passion. But she was definitely in lust with Jack Stone. And yes, when she was in his arms, she became uncontrollable with passion. She could hardly wait for tonight to come.

'I have some photos of it, if you'd like to look at them,' Vivienne offered. Perhaps unwisely, as it turned out. Because she couldn't look at the various rooms without thinking of what they'd done in them, espe-cially that spare bedroom with that old brass bed in it.

'It's going to be a big job,' Marion said. 'You'll be away for weeks. Maybe even months!'

'Possibly,' Vivienne agreed, all the while thinking she didn't care how long it would take.

Marion gave her one of her rather sharp looks. It was hard to put something over on Marion. She was very good at reading between the lines.

'I was somewhat surprised by Jack Stone,' she said. 'He wasn't nearly the ogre you've painted him out to be. I rather liked him.'

'Yes, well, he can be quite nice when he wants something from you,' she said drily. Which was very true.

'He's also better looking than I thought he'd be,' Marion added.

'He's passable, I suppose,' Vivienne said offhandedly as she sipped her coffee.

'More than passable. But then, he's my type. I've always liked manly men. My Bob was a manly man,' Marion said in that wistful tone which warned Vivienne Marion was about to get maudlin over her long-dead husband. Normally, Vivienne didn't mind listening to Marion's memories of happier times, but not today. She didn't want to hear about what true love felt like. And she didn't want to think about lost loves.

Her phone ringing at that point was a blessed distraction until she picked it up and saw it was Jack calling. From the frying pan into the fire, she thought as her heart started racing and her head worried about Marion twigging what was going on between them.

'Hello,' she said, deliberately leaving out Jack's name.

'And hello back,' he said. 'Did you sleep well? I know I did.'

Vivienne could see Marion looking at her with curiosity in her eyes.

'It's Jack,' she mouthed, as though it was nothing.

'How nice of you to get back to me so quickly about the door,' she said aloud to him.

Jack got the message straight away. 'Ah...you have someone with you. Marion, I presume?'

'Wow, that *was* quick,' she said and he laughed. 'So I can expect the man to come with the new door tomorrow,' she went on in a matter-of-fact tone. 'What time?'

'Well, certainly not at seven in the morning,' he said.

'You'll be too wrecked to get up that early after what I have in mind for you tonight.'

Vivienne swallowed convulsively as she struggled not to blush. But, oh, the heat which immediately flooded her body at his highly provocative words…

'Noon will be fine,' she said, amazed at how cool and calm she actually sounded. Who would have imagined she could be such a good actress? 'Thank you, Jack. And thank you again for offering me such a wonderful job. I'm looking forward to it.'

He laughed again. 'Not as much as I am, Miss Cool. Now, as much as I am enjoying this titillating conversation, I have to go now. Work calls. I'll pick you up at seven tonight. And don't wear anything too sexy, if you want to pass it off as a business dinner.'

Vivienne opened her mouth to reply but he'd already hung up. Which was just as well, with Marion listening avidly.

'Fine,' she said into the dead phone. 'Thank you again. Goodbye.'

'I think he likes you,' Marion said straight away.

Vivienne put her phone back down on the table before answering.

'What makes you say that?'

'Feminine instinct. I mean, he could have employed any competent interior designer to do up this house of his, but he came looking specifically for you.'

As much as there was a part of Vivienne which was flattered by the truth in Marion's statement, she wasn't about to fall victim to thinking Jack had had anything but work in mind when he'd come in search of her the other day. What had happened between them was as unexpected to him as it was to her.

'Yes, well, he knows my work, doesn't he? He knows

I'll do a good job.' *And you'll give him good head at the same time,* came the truly wicked thought.

Vivienne still could not believe how much she liked doing that. It was a mystery all right. But Jack's motivations weren't a mystery. He was a typical man who could enjoy sex without having his heart involved. Yes, he liked her, but he didn't care for her to any great degree. He certainly didn't love her. And she was strangely comfortable with that. Sleeping together whilst they worked together was as much a bonus for her as it was for him. She refused to feel guilty about it any more. Or to continue to worry that she was on some kind of perverse rebound trip.

'I'm still not convinced,' Marion said. 'And you know what? I think you like him back.'

Vivienne smiled at her. 'Hard not to like a man who brought me flowers then gave me such a dream job.' *Not to mention countless orgasms.* 'But you're right. I do like him a lot better now than I did.'

'Hmm. He's single, isn't he?'

'Yes. And wants to stay that way.'

'Does he have a girlfriend?'

What to say to that? 'Yes, he does,' she said at last. Impossible to use the word 'mistress'.

'Oh. Pity. What's she like, do you know?'

'Not really. I've only met her the once.' Yesterday, when she'd been suddenly transformed into Vivienne the Vamp.

'Is she blonde?'

'No. A redhead.'

'Oh. Like you. Beautiful? Sexy?'

Vivienne shrugged. 'I dare say Jack thinks so.'

'But you don't.'

'She's okay, I guess. She's a working girl. A designer,

like me. Jack met her through work.' Lord, this word game she was playing was getting a bit complicated. Vivienne wished now she hadn't started it.

Marion snorted. 'I suppose she's hoping he falls in love with her and marries her in the end.'

Vivienne almost laughed, because nothing could have been further from the truth. But she could hardly say that.

'I suppose so,' she said. 'Most women want love and marriage.' *But not me. Not right now, anyway. I just want lots of great sex. With Jack.*

Marion was frowning. 'If she's a designer, why didn't Jack ask her to redecorate Francesco's Folly?'

Vivienne had to think quickly. 'I guess he didn't want her to get ideas about it becoming their future home together. Jack told me yesterday that he bought it on impulse when he was up that way, looking for land for a retirement village. I think he wants it as his secret hideaway.'

'I see,' Marion mused aloud. 'Yes, I see. Jack's really not going to marry her then, is he? Poor thing. She's going to get her heart broken if she's not careful.'

No, I won't, Vivienne thought with a stab of surprising certainty. *What I'm doing with Jack has nothing to do with my heart. It's not a love affair. It's a fling; that's all it is. A strictly sexual fling.*

'She's the sort of girl who can take care of herself,' Vivienne said firmly as she stood up and carried the now empty mugs over to the sink. Which was true— most of the time. She'd been taking care of herself for as long as she could remember. Not by choice, by necessity. Independence and self-sufficiency had become an ingrained habit. So had emotional toughness.

Until she'd met Daryl, that was. He'd wormed his

way under her skin and through the hard shell she'd encased her heart in. Her love for him had made her act in ways which were uncharacteristic and unwise. Being with him had made her weak. And blind.

Jack had been right when he'd said it was a good thing that she hadn't married Daryl. It was. He would have been a horrible husband, and she a pathetic wife. His betrayal still hurt when she thought about it. But not as much as it had. Perhaps because she didn't think about it as much any more.

'You're thinking about Daryl, aren't you?' Marion said intuitively from where she was still sitting at the kitchen table.

Vivienne turned from the sink and looked over at her friend. 'Who?' she said with brilliant nonchalance.

Marion laughed. 'Now, that's a step in the right direction.'

CHAPTER FOURTEEN

JACK JUMPED OUT of his Porsche at twenty past seven, annoyed that he was late picking up Vivienne. He hated being late, especially tonight. But one couldn't always control the traffic. He hoped she wouldn't be angry with him.

Her smiling face when she opened the door was reassuring.

'You're late,' she chided him. But gently.

'There was a breakdown on the bridge,' he explained. 'Sorry.'

'No need to apologise. I understand. I'll just get my purse and lock up.'

Perversely, Jack felt irritated by her casual acceptance of his tardiness. If she'd been looking forward to tonight as much as he was, she would have been more upset. But of course, she wasn't emotionally involved with him, was she? He was just a male body to her. A bed partner with whom she could play erotic games. She didn't want to be his girlfriend. She preferred the role of mistress. It was stupid of him to want more from her when it was obvious she was incapable of giving him more at this time in her life. He should just take what he could get and, when the time came, walk away.

Clenching his teeth hard in his jaw, Jack determined

to treat her the way she wanted to be treated—as nothing more than a sex object. A plaything. His own personal *Penthouse* Pet. There would be no pity for her. Or mercy.

Which meant dinner would definitely not be lingered over. He wanted her back in his bed as soon as possible.

So, as she walked back down the hallway towards him, he let his eyes travel slowly over her from top to toe, not bothering to hide his lecherous intent. She hadn't obeyed his command not to dress sexily, he noted, which puzzled him slightly. If she didn't want anyone to guess at the true nature of their relationship, she should have worn something less...provocative.

Her dress was purple, a wrap-around, figure-hugging style which showed off her hourglass shape in a way which did little to dampen his desire for her. Her hair was up, but in a softly sexy style, with tendrils hanging around her lovely face. She was wearing more eye make-up than usual, making her green eyes look huge. As for her glossed lips...they looked downright wicked. And then there were the earrings, long crystal drops which drew the eye down to her impressive cleavage.

'I told you not to wear anything sexy,' he said brusquely once she was close enough to touch.

She shrugged her slender shoulders. 'I decided a mistress wouldn't go out with her lover looking dreary.'

'True,' he said, and without asking her permission swept her into his arms and kissed her.

Vivienne only resisted for a second or two, and then only because of shock at his sudden move. This was what she wanted, after all—to be in his arms again. To feel the heat of his flesh pressed hard against hers. And his body *was* hard. Hard all over.

Soon, she didn't even want to go to dinner. If he'd

pushed her back inside and into her bedroom, she would not have objected.

If only she hadn't dropped her keys onto the wooden floorboards.

His head lifted abruptly at the clattering sound, giving her a wry look before bending down to pick them up. Vivienne clenched the offending hands as she tried to regain control over herself. Her face felt hot and her whole body was in danger of imminent meltdown. She could not speak. Could hardly think. After straightening, he took a closer look at her and smiled a smile which she couldn't fathom. Was it amusement curving his lips? Or some strange kind of satisfaction?

'I'll lock up for you,' he said.

She just stared at him, her head slowly clearing from the fog of passion which had been clouding her normally sharp brain. Not for the first time, she wondered why Jack aroused her so easily to a level of lust which was both overpowering and overwhelming. One kiss and she was his again. Instantly. Being his beck-and-call girl was never going to present a problem. Because she wanted to do everything with him, and for him.

Sexually speaking, that was. She especially liked it when he was masterful with her. When he was demanding. When he took without asking. How strange was that? She'd always hated domineering, arrogant men. Yet she didn't hate Jack. If truth be told, she liked him even more than she'd admitted to Marion. She was also finding him more handsome than she ever had before.

Of course, he was dressed more smartly than usual tonight in a dark grey suit, white shirt and a blue tie the colour of his eyes. A man was always improved when wearing a suit, she thought, especially suits as well-fitting as Jack's. It gave him an air of urbane sophistication which she hadn't seen in him before. She'd always thought of Jack as a rough diamond; he was anything but rough in that extremely elegant suit.

He turned and caught her staring at him.

But he didn't say anything, just handed her the keys and took her arm, leading her outside.

It was cooler than she'd expected after the warmth of the day. Vivienne ground to a halt before they reached the pavement.

'I think I should go back and get a jacket,' she told Jack. Her dress did have three-quarter sleeves but the material was thin.

'Absolutely not,' he replied firmly. 'No covering up for you tonight, beautiful.'

Vivienne winced. 'Would you mind not calling me that? I really don't like it.'

His facial muscles tightened. 'What shall I call you, then? Sweetheart? Honey? Surely not darling? That doesn't seem to befit a mistress.'

Vivienne's hand clutched her purse tightly within angry fingers. 'Why are you acting like a jerk all of a sudden?' she threw at him.

He glared at her for a moment, then sighed, his face softening. 'You're right. I am acting like a jerk. Blame it on male ego. I'm still smarting over your not wanting to be my girlfriend for real.'

Vivienne was tempted to give in and say, *okay, I'll be your girlfriend for real*. Because she didn't like to think he was angry with her. But she seriously didn't want to do that. She knew she would regret it afterwards if she gave in.

'You seemed happy with our arrangement when you dropped me off last night,' she reminded him tautly.

'Besides, I thought a strictly sexual relationship would be right up your alley.'

'So did I.'

'Then what's your problem?'

Yeah, Jack, what's your problem? For pity's sake, get a grip.

He shrugged. 'No real problem. But perhaps you could compromise a little and go out with me occasionally. On a proper date, that is.'

'That's what I'm doing tonight, isn't it?'

He laughed. 'You and I both know that tonight's dinner is just foreplay, not a date. Hell, I took one look at you in that dress and instantly decided to reduce the meal to only one course. You're going to be my dessert, gorgeous. Can I call you that—gorgeous?'

'If you must,' she said, struggling to keep her own desire in check.

'Good. So let's stop this useless banter and be on our way. The quicker we get there and eat, the quicker we can leave.'

But it didn't turn out quite that way. Shortly after they were shown to a table in the small Italian restaurant Jack had booked in nearby St Leonards, his phone pinged.

'Sorry,' he said as he whipped the infernal thing out of his pocket. 'Have to have a quick look to see. It could be family.'

As much as Vivienne admired Jack's devotion to his family, she wished he'd left his phone at home—like she had. But she supposed that was being irrational. And more like a girlfriend's thinking than a mistress's. A mistress would not object to her wealthy lover doing anything at all, even answering text messages when he was at dinner with her.

Jack's frown as he read the message aroused Vivienne's curiosity.

'Something wrong?' she prompted.

He put the phone back in his pocket. 'No. Not really. It was an invite to an engagement party next week.'

'Oh? Who's getting married? Family or friends?'

'Neither. It's the daughter of a business acquaintance. A very wealthy business acquaintance.'

'So you're probably wise to attend.'

'I'm not sure that would be wise. I might punch out the groom-to-be.'

Vivienne was taken aback. 'Why on earth would you do that?'

His smile was very droll. 'His name is Daryl.'

The waiter bringing the bottle of wine Jack had ordered stopped Vivienne from saying or doing anything at that precise moment that she would regret. It also gave her a minute or two to gather herself, and her thoughts.

It was only natural, she accepted once she could think properly, that Frank Ellison would invite Jack to Courtney's engagement party. Jack had, after all, built Frank's harbourside mansion, the same one she had decorated last year. Had she received an invitation too? Vivienne wondered. She doubted it. As much as Frank might be ignorant of Daryl's very recent engagement to another woman, Courtney certainly wasn't. Or was she? Maybe the girl didn't know he'd been engaged when they'd started seeing each other.

Vivienne suppressed a sigh. She didn't want to think about Daryl any more, or the new life he'd made for himself with Courtney Ellison. She'd moved on and, although his actions had hurt her badly, she was feeling better now. Much, much better.

By the time the waiter poured the wine, took their

dinner orders and departed, Vivienne knew what she had to do.

First she lifted her glass of chilled Chardonnay to her lips and took a deep swallow. Then she locked eyes with Jack over the rim and said in steely tones, 'I presume your invitation says "and partner"?'

Jack had an awful feeling he knew what was coming.

'Yes,' he answered warily.

'In that case, I'd like to come with you.'

He *knew* it! Jack sighed his frustration. 'I really don't think that's a good idea, Vivienne.'

Her eyes turned mutinous. 'Why?' she snapped.

'Because you don't know what and who you're dealing with,' he shot back just as sharply.

'Yes I do. I'm dealing with a two-timing bastard who's been allowed to get away with his disgusting behaviour up till now,' she said, doing her best to keep her voice low so that the other people in the restaurant didn't overhear. 'He lied to me when he broke off our engagement. Claimed he hadn't been unfaithful, that he was doing the honourable thing by leaving me before sleeping with his new love. And I actually believed him at the time! My God, I can't believe I was such a gullible little fool where that man was concerned.

'The moment I saw those photos in the paper, I should have gone after him and told him what I thought of him. I should have made him suffer a little, even if it was only discomfort at the distress he'd caused. This is the perfect opportunity for me to confront him. Look, for all I know, Courtney Ellison might not even know about his engagement to me. Daryl could have lied to her as well. I want to make sure she is well aware of what kind of man she's planning to marry!'

'There's no chance in hell that Courtney doesn't

already know everything about you, Vivienne,' Jack stated with bald honesty. 'Trust me when I say that Daryl being engaged to you would have added to his attraction for her. Seduction is her favourite game. She went after me big time when I was building her father's house and cornered me in one of the home's ten bed-rooms one day, as naked as a jay bird.'

Vivienne's eyes had gone wide, showing Jack how shocked she was, her reaction to such behaviour un-derlining to him that she would never do such a thing. This strictly sexual fling she was having with him…it was definitely out of character for her. She was the kind of girl who would usually want marriage and children, not the role of mistress.

'Heavens!' she exclaimed, shaking her head. 'And did you…did you…?'

'No. I wouldn't touch Courtney Ellison with a barge pole,' he ground out.

Was that relief he saw in her eyes? He sure hoped so. Because that would show that she genuinely liked him, the way he liked her.

'You don't want to be around people like that if you don't have to be, Vivienne,' he went on. 'They're bad, greedy, soulless people. You're way too good for them. Like I said, you're much better off without someone like Daryl in your life.'

'I dare say what you've just said is all true. But, on a personal level, I need to show Daryl that I've survived. That he didn't destroy me. If I go to their party with you, it will be the perfect revenge.'

All the breath left Jack's lungs at the word 'revenge'. God, but that actually hurt. He leant back in his chair and studied her for a few moments. 'Is that all I am to you, Vivienne?' he asked quietly. 'An instrument of revenge?'

'What? No, no, of course not. How can you possibly say that after all I've done with you? None of that was revenge. It was…it was… Well, it was just lust,' she finished, her face flushed and flustered.

'Just lust,' he repeated, not feeling particularly happy with that little phrase either. Though it was a lot better than revenge.

'Jack, trust me, I am over Daryl, and our sexual relationship has nothing to do with him.'

'Can't say I'm convinced, but I'll take you to the party if that's what you really want.'

'That's what I really want,' she told him.

'In that case, I have one proviso.'

'What?'

'Once you've shown your face and had your say, we leave straight away. I have no intention of spending my leisure time with people like that. I'd much rather be somewhere else. With my gorgeous mistress,' he added, then smiled at her.

CHAPTER FIFTEEN

JACK'S WICKEDLY SEXY smile did things to Vivienne which were even more wicked. It constantly amazed Vivienne how quickly Jack could turn her on. A moment ago, her mind had been focused on what she would say and do at Daryl's engagement party. A split second later, she could think of nothing but being with Jack, her body liquefying as various erotic images danced in her head.

Time to go to the ladies' room, she decided, making her excuses just as the waiter arrived with a plate of delicious looking herb-and-garlic bread.

'Don't be too long,' Jack said as he reached for a slice. 'Or this will all be gone.'

She wasn't long. Just long enough to cool her overheated body, and to change her mind about going to Courtney Ellison's engagement party. It surprised Vivienne to find that she cared about Jack's feelings more than her own need to confront Daryl. She hated Jack thinking that she was using him for revenge. Because she wasn't.

'You'll be pleased to know,' she said as she sat down again and reached for one of the two remaining slices of bread, 'that I've decided not to go to that party after all.'

Jack did not seem as pleased as she thought he'd be.

'Oh? And why's that?'

'You obviously don't want to take me. And I don't want to risk spoiling what we have together.'

His eyebrows lifted.

'Look, Daryl's dead and gone as far as I'm concerned,' she went on firmly. 'Let's leave him that way.'

Jack didn't believe that for a moment. Darling Daryl wasn't dead and gone in Vivienne's mind. He was still there, influencing everything she did. His dumping her so cruelly for another woman was undoubtedly one of the reasons she'd jumped into *his* bed. Maybe not out of revenge, but there had to be an element of rebound in her actions. Okay, so there was lust, too—though Jack preferred to think of it as passion and need. Vivienne was obviously a highly sexed girl who enjoyed making love in all its forms. No doubt she'd always had a very active and imaginative sex life with Daryl.

Damn it all, but he didn't like thinking about her doing the things with that bastard that she'd done with him!

Still, her being so darned sexy was one of the things he liked about her. That and her undeniable strength of character and courage. If she really wanted to go to that party then who was he to say no?

'I appreciate your concerns, Vivienne,' he said. 'And I love it that you don't want to risk spoiling our relationship.' *Such as it is,* he thought ruefully. 'But I've had a few moments to think about the situation from your point of view and I now believe it *would* be a good idea to go to that party. Otherwise, you'll never have closure on the matter. You need to have the opportunity to tell your ex what you think of him. And prove to yourself that you're not a coward,' he added for good measure.

He'd surprised her. No doubt about that.

'Then you're happy to take me?'

'Absolutely. Ah, here's our dinner.'

Vivienne had actually forgotten what kind of spaghetti Jack had ordered, her mind having been elsewhere when they'd first arrived at the restaurant. Fortunately, she was not a fussy eater and she loved Italian food. The plate of spaghetti marinara placed before her was a huge serving, with a wide variety of seafood as well as the fish pieces: mussels; prawns; scallops; calamari.

'Goodness!' she exclaimed as she picked up her fork. 'It'll take me all night to eat this.'

'I sincerely hope not.'

Vivienne's stomach did a little somersault. She knew exactly what he was referring to and the thought excited her unbearably. Dear heaven, she was turning into a sex addict. She had to do something, *say* something to get her mind off the subject.

'Jack,' she said abruptly.

He swallowed a mussel with relish before looking up at her. 'Yep?' he said, and dabbed at his mouth with a serviette.

Oh, God. Why did he have to do that? She stared at his somewhat hard mouth and thought of the pleasure it gave her. *All* of it: lips; teeth; tongue. But especially his tongue. She could feel it now, licking, stabbing, sliding inside her.

The heat her thoughts evoked made her squeeze her thighs and buttocks tightly together. Dear heaven, she almost came then. Putting down her fork, she straightened her spine against the back of the chair, forcing herself to get a firm grip on her wayward flesh.

'I was wondering if you'd heard anything more about Francesco's Folly today?' she asked, always having found work a welcome distraction when her emotions threatened to get out of hand. 'Do you know when I might be able to move in there and start work?'

'Good news there. Things should be finalised by the end of next week. You can move in as soon as you like after that.'

'And my contract?'

'I'll draw one up for you before that. Which reminds me—I've contacted a builder I know who's going to do the actual work. He's reliable and has lots of contacts in the area. Knows all the local tradies and building suppliers. I've been wondering, since you'll be living on site, if you'd take on the job as project manager as well as interior decorator? I'll pay extra, of course,' he added, and forked in another mouthful of seafood.

'How much extra?'

He smiled. 'Lots.'

'Okay,' she said with a shrug which belied her crippling sexual tension. Talking about work hadn't distracted her at all!

'Good. Now, eat up. Nothing worse than cold pasta.'

She did her best. But her appetite still lay elsewhere. She watched Jack tuck into his meal with relish whilst only picking at hers. She did eat the seafood, the pasta part remaining untouched. And she did drink the wine. Most of the bottle; Jack told her he never had more than one glass when driving. By the time Jack pushed his own empty plate aside, the alcohol had driven out any feelings of nerves, leaving her with nothing but the most dizzying need.

'Not hungry?' he said as he wiped his mouth again with his serviette.

Vivienne swallowed the last mouthful of wine. 'Not really,' she said.

'Do you want anything more to drink? A Cognac? Coffee?'

'No, thanks.'

He looked hard at her, then nodded.

'Fine,' he said, and waved the waiter over.

Five minutes later they were out in the very cool night air, Vivienne shivering as Jack took her elbow and steered her towards the small car park behind the restaurant. His Porsche was parked over in a dimly lit corner, next to a red Mercedes.

'You must be cold,' he said, walking quickly.

Vivienne wouldn't have been as cold if she hadn't felt so hot. She frowned when he steered her round to the driver's side into the small gap between the car and a solid wooden fence.

'This'll have to do,' he said gruffly, and pushed her back up against the car door. 'I can't wait till we get back to my place, Vivienne. You must know that. Drop that bag and kick off your shoes,' he ordered her in a low, gravelly voice.

She did so, then stood there, still shivering, with her back against the car whilst his hands scooped up under her skirt and yanked both her panties and tights down in one rough movement. They joined her bag on the ground.

'Hold your skirt up to your waist,' he commanded.

She did so, shocked by her blind obedience to him. She heard voices nearby, but she knew she wouldn't drop her skirt. Not unless he told her to. Which he didn't. He just stared at her, then touched her between her quivering thighs, pushing them aside, then delving into the hot, wet core of her sex. She moaned softly, then not so softly. Thank God the voices had gone, because the whole world could have come to watch her and she would not have stopped.

She was perilously close to coming when he stopped and dropped to his knees before her. With a strangled cry she spread her legs wider, her knees bending slightly to give his mouth better access to her by then desperate body. The feel of his tongue stabbing mercilessly against her throbbing clitoris was more than she could bear, and she was unable to smother the tortured cry of release which immediately erupted from her panting mouth.

The next few seconds were a blur. Vivienne was thankful for the car's support or she might have sunk to the ground. She wasn't aware of Jack's actions, having squeezed her eyes tightly shut against the shattering storm of her climax. Just when she thought she might live, she felt Jack enter her, then surge upwards. Her eyes shot open and she stared into his flushed face. His eyes were wild, his mouth twisted, the urgency of his own need very obvious.

When he lifted her up she automatically wrapped her legs around his hips, her hands letting go of her skirt so that she could wind her arms around his neck. Her dress fell down over them like a curtain. Not that what they were doing was subtle. Anyone walking by would have known instantly what was happening.

He groaned as he ground slowly into her, his hands kneading her buttocks at the same time.

But she didn't want him slow. She wanted him hard. And fast.

'Faster, Jack,' she urged, squeezing him tightly with her insides.

'Bloody hell, Vivienne,' he muttered, taking a bruising grip of her hips before grinding into her with a power which took her breath away. He came almost as quickly as she had, shuddering into her, groaning his satisfaction. Vivienne didn't mind that she was left still wanting. Jack's pleasure was enough for her at the moment.

She began to shiver when he lowered her to the ground, the heat of the moment giving way to the chill of the night.

He shook his head at her. 'We're mad. You do know that, don't you?'

'Yes,' she agreed shakily. 'Quite mad.'

'Anyone could have come.'

'I didn't care.'

'I know. Neither did I. Come on, let's get you into the warmth of the car. You'll catch your death if we stay out here.'

'Well, there's one consolation,' he added wryly, once they were under way with the heater going full blast.

'What's that?' she asked somewhat dazedly. She was, quite frankly, still a little off the planet.

'I had enough of a brain left to use a condom.'

'Yes. Yes, I noticed that,' she said. But only after he withdrew. She hadn't during the act. She'd been off in another world. It was just as well she was on the pill. Being with Jack had made her uncharacteristically reckless. He wasn't much better. They were mad, all right. Mad for each other. She almost told him then that she was on the pill because of course it would be better, not having to worry about protection all the time, especially if they were going to have spontaneous sex at any given moment. Which seemed on the cards. His desire for her was as strong as hers for him. But being on the pill only protected you against pregnancy, nothing else. She couldn't see Jack as a man who took silly risks, but who knew?

'What are you thinking about?' he asked her when they stopped at a set of lights.

'Nothing.'

'Come now, Vivienne, I know you too well. Your mind is never empty.'

She stared down at the bag in her lap which was bulging from where she'd stuffed in her cotton panties. The tights, she'd left behind since they'd been ruined when Jack had ripped them off her. Finally, she looked up and over at him.

'I was thinking I'm going to go out tomorrow and buy myself some seriously sexy underwear,' she invented. 'As long as you promise not to destroy it, that is.'

He smiled a wicked little smile. 'Sorry. Can't give you any guarantees on that. You bring out the beast in me.'

'I do?'

'You know you do.'

'You bring out the same in me,' she admitted. 'I'm not usually like this, you know.'

'What do you mean?' he asked straight away.

Vivienne wished she hadn't said that. For how could she tell him that she'd never before done a tenth of the things that she'd done with him? He probably wouldn't believe her. Either that or he'd start asking her questions, questions she didn't have answers for. She didn't want to think about why she was so different with him. She just wanted to live in the moment. To say and do whatever she wanted with him. To be wild and wanton and, yes, even downright wicked.

She smiled a saucy smile. 'I mean, I don't usually have sex in car parks. But it was fun, wasn't it?'

His smile was wry. 'It wouldn't have been fun if we'd been arrested.'

'Can you get arrested for that?'

'I would imagine so.'

'Have you ever been arrested?' she asked, happy to change the subject from herself onto him.

'Not as yet.' The lights went green and he drove on towards the bridge. 'You're coming back to my place for the night, aren't you?'

'What…the whole night?' She hadn't been expecting that. But instantly, it was what she wanted to do. To sleep with him naked, all night, where she could touch him at will, kiss him all over, whenever and wherever it took her fancy.

'You have a problem with that?' he said when she remained silent. Little did he know the thoughts going on in her head, or the instant need gripping her flesh. 'I could drop you home first thing in the morning on my way to work. You could sneak in like a naughty teenager before Marion wakes up and spots you.'

'Marion never wakes up till around ten,' she told him, her matter-of-fact tone hiding the escalating desire firing her blood once more. 'Not when she's doing the two-to-ten shift. She doesn't get home till nearly eleven, and she's always dog tired. She never knocks on my door till late morning.'

'That settles it, then. You're staying the night.'

'If that's what you want,' she agreed, hugging her excitement to herself.

Jack glanced over at her and wondered what she'd been really thinking back at the lights. He wasn't a mind reader—especially where women were concerned— but he doubted she'd been thinking about underwear shopping.

Vivienne was an enigma all right. Always cool on the surface, but underneath, very hot to trot, a classic case of fire and ice. His stomach lurched when he thought of how she'd urged him on back in that car park.

'Faster, Jack,' she'd said in a voice unlike the one she used when working. Or even just now, here, in the car. There'd been nothing cool, calm and collected about that voice. It had been wild!

He felt the sex between them now would be even better, knowing he had all night. He could take his time with her. Make her wait more. Make her see the rapture in elongated foreplay. There was something infinitely satisfying about long, slow lovemaking where the emphasis was not so much on coming but on sensual experiences. He would stroke her back with gentle hands, massage her bottom with oil and caress her beautiful breasts. He would make her sigh with pleasure. He wanted to satisfy her more completely than she'd ever been satisfied before.

'Now what are *you* thinking?' she asked.

Jack turned to smile at her. 'I was thinking that you don't need to buy any new underwear. Because, from now on, you won't be wearing any.'

Her blush startled Jack. Why on earth, he wondered, would the girl who'd just done what she'd just done blush at the idea of going without her underwear? It didn't compute. She was an enigma all right. A woman of contradictions and contrary behaviour.

Take her apartment, for instance. Why was it furnished in such a stark way when her professional designs were never like that? Vivienne had a reputation for creating warm, comfy interiors which appealed to people. It was why he always hired her to do his show units and villas, because her décor made them sell. There had to be reasons for why she'd chosen to decorate her own place in such a soulless fashion; deep, personal reasons. Jack suspected it had something to do with her family background, which obviously hadn't been very happy. She'd sounded stressed when she'd talked about her parents. She hadn't been all that forthcoming, either. Most of the women he'd dated in the past were eager to talk about themselves, launching into detailed life stories without too much encouragement.

Of course, he wasn't *dating* Vivienne, was he? He was just sleeping with her. For now, that was. Jack hadn't abandoned his idea of her becoming his girlfriend for real. He'd just put it on the back-burner for a while.

One day, in the hopefully not-too-distant future, she would see that it would be good for her to date a guy like him: an honest, straightforward, straight-down-the-line type of guy who didn't lie or cheat and who could show her a good time, in bed and out, without any false declarations of love and till-death-do-us-part commitment. Just the thing she needed after getting tangled up with El Creepo. And, when she finally realised that having an easygoing boyfriend would be good for her—*and* once she got her trust back in men—he would find out all that she'd been hiding from him.

Meanwhile, he would give her exactly what she wanted. Which was fine by him, because quite frankly, right at this moment, it was just what he wanted as well.

CHAPTER SIXTEEN

'It's amazing he could find a door to match your old one,' Marion said as she looked at Vivienne's new bathroom door. 'Amazing that the man came on time to do it as well,' she added.

'Jack said all his contractors come on time,' Vivienne said, very happy with the door. It had even been painted the same colour, Bert explaining that he'd taken a scraping of the paint when he'd come to look at it the first time. It had only taken him half an hour to remove the old door and put in the new one. Marion had dropped in once she'd seen Bert drive off.

'In that case I'll certainly be giving Jack a ring if ever I want something fixed. Tradies give me the willies, the way they're never reliable.'

'I know what you mean. Jack won't tolerate workers who are late, or unreliable, or don't do things up to his high standards.'

'Hmm. A difficult man to work for, then,' Marion said.

'Difficult. And demanding,' Vivienne agreed. 'But fair.'

'Still, make sure you get a proper contract with him. You can't be too trusting, even if Jack is normally a fair man. He might try to get you to do this job under the table, so to speak. You know, cash in hand. There's no security in that. Where money is concerned, even the fairest man might be tempted to take advantage. And you're vulnerable at the moment, Vivienne, even more vulnerable in the coming weeks without me around to warn you to be careful. Jack didn't get to be as success-ful as he is without being a bit ruthless on occasion.'

'Don't worry. I won't let him take advantage of me. But, might I remind you that you never warned me about Daryl?'

Marion sighed. 'I have to confess that Daryl took me in as well, the handsome devil. He was an accom-plished charmer all right. Though, looking back, I sup-pose he was always too good to be true. Too ready with the compliments, if you know what I mean.'

'Yes. Yes, I certainly do know what you mean,' Vivi-enne said, recalling how over the top he'd been in his praise of her. Not just her looks but other things, things which she knew weren't true. But she'd lapped it up all the same, thinking he was praising her out of love, imagining that he'd been *blinded* by loved, whereas in fact *she'd* been the one who'd been blinded.

Jack, on other hand, was thankfully light on the com-pliments. Yes, he'd called her beautiful and gorgeous at times, but that was par for the course with men who wanted to have sex with you. And, yes, when in bed he did say nice things about her body. Especially her breasts and her bottom. But he didn't rave on at length, for which she was grateful.

What he did at length—last night especially—was make love to her. Impossible to call it anything else this time, Vivienne conceded Jack had showed her that sex with him didn't have to be kinky or quick or in unusual places and positions to be stunningly pleasurable. He'd surprised her with how long he could spend on fore-play, caressing, admiring and gently exploring every inch of her body before finally entering her, where he rocked gently back and forth, kissing her every so often, bringing her ever so slowly to climax in the most sat-isfying way.

Then, after a short rest during which they'd lain in each other's arms and talked about what plans they had for Francesco's Folly, he'd made love to her again. Once again he'd been in no hurry, remaining still inside her for ages whilst he'd played with her breasts and told her how lovely they were, and that he could stay doing what he was doing for ever. Which was what it seemed like he did, in hindsight.

Vivienne knew she should have been exhausted today. Instead, she felt more alive than she ever had before. She could hardly wait to see Jack again tonight.

'I have to go get ready for work,' Marion said, break-ing into Vivienne's thoughts. 'Now, forget all about das-tardly Daryl. He's not worth thinking about. See you tomorrow, love.'

Marion's advice reminded Vivienne of her decision to go to Daryl's engagement party. Once again, she no longer felt as strongly about doing so. If truth be told, Daryl was fading from her mind. Yes, it still stung, what he'd done. And yes, he didn't deserve to get away with it scot free. But would she really have the gall to con-front him at his engagement party? It *would* take cour-age; she could see that now. Jack hadn't wanted her to go at first, then he'd said he did. Something about clo-sure—he was probably right. She supposed she could do it, with him by her side. He wouldn't let anything horrible happen to her. Of that Vivienne felt confident. He was a man who could be relied upon.

Vivienne reached out to pull the bathroom door shut, pleased that it didn't stick the way the other one had. She smiled. Oh, yes, Jack could be relied on. She wondered if she should text him, tell him that the door man had come and done a splendid job. Yes, of course she could. He wouldn't mind. But she wouldn't ring. He'd told her he didn't like to be rung when he was at work, not unless there was an emergency. Which there wasn't. But she did so want to contact him. It would be like touching him. She did so like touching him. With a shiver of remembered pleasure, she hurried out to the kitchen where she'd left her phone.

'Marion says I'm to make sure I get a proper contract with you,' Vivienne told Jack later that night. They were in his very nice bed in his very nice apartment, lying in each other's arms in a state of post-coital bliss. 'She says I'm not to let you take advantage of me, and then she warned me that you must be ruthless to become as successful in business as you have.'

Jack's eyebrows lifted. 'And do you agree with her? About my being ruthless?'

'Not really. No, I don't think you're ruthless. You are a tough man to deal with on a professional basis, but fair. And I told her so. You'll be glad to know, however, that I didn't inform her that on the personal side you're a bit of a softie.'

Jack laughed. 'That's not what you said a few minutes ago. You said I was hard as a rock.'

She gave him a playful slap on his magnificent chest. 'Don't be silly. You know what I mean. I was talking about the way you love your family, especially your mother. A man who loves his mother couldn't be bad.'

'Really? I seem to recall reading somewhere that Hitler loved his mother.'

She glowered up at him. 'You just made that up.'

He faked a shocked expression. 'You don't think I read?'

'I didn't say that.'

'I'll have you know I read all the time. Only yesterday I picked up a copy of *Playboy* at a building site and read it from cover to cover. *Very* interesting articles in that magazine.'

Now it was Vivienne's turn to laugh. 'I'll bet. No seriously, do you like to read? Because I do. Very much.'

'Can't say it's my favourite pastime,' he admitted.

'I couldn't be without a book. I read every night before I go to sleep. Or I used to,' she added, thinking she hadn't read a word since she'd started her relationship with Jack. He left her exhausted naturally after their passionate nights together.

'If that's the case, how come you don't have bookshelves crammed with books in your place? Or do you keep them all under your bed? I haven't been in there yet.'

And neither will you, Vivienne thought with a spurt of panic. She didn't want to be with him in the same bed she'd shared with Daryl. A small part of her was still afraid that if she did that she might revert to being the same pathetic bed partner she'd been with him, something which still occasionally bothered and confused her. If she'd loved Daryl—truly loved him—why hadn't she been more passionate with him? Why hadn't she enjoyed sex with him the way she did with Jack? There was no making sense of it. Really, there wasn't.

'I don't keep the books I read,' she told Jack in answer to his question. 'I buy a couple at a time from a

local second-hand bookshop and when I finish reading them I return them and get two more. No point in
keeping them after I've read them, is there?' she said,
and glanced up at him.

Jack shrugged. 'I don't know. You could always lend
them to friends. Doesn't Marion read?'

'Yes, but not the kind of books I read. She likes romance and I like crime.'

'I see,' Jack said. 'I like watching crime shows on
TV,' he ventured.

'I do, too. Which ones are your favourite?' she asked,
and they talked at some length about their favourite pro-
grammes, Jack discovering that Vivienne liked shows
which mixed crime with relationships, not just crime
itself.

'So you do like some romance in your stories,' he
said at last. 'Just so long as it's not *all* romance.'

'Yes. Yes, I suppose that's true.'

'Now, you told me earlier that you were driving Marion to the airport on Saturday, is that right?'

'Yes.'

'What time?'

'Around one. Her plane goes just after three.'

'And will you stay with her till the plane leaves?'

'Yes, I thought I would. I couldn't let her go off
alone.'

'Yes, of course. I'm not complaining. I'm just trying to work out the weekend. I was originally going to
suggest we drive up to Francesco's Folly on Saturday
and stay the night but that's not very practical when
you probably won't be back from the airport till after
four. I'll go visit Mum instead on Saturday whilst you're
busy. Then I'll take you out somewhere special for dinner that night. If you want to go, of course,' he added,

adhering to her rule that he asked her first. 'Then, if you like, you could stay the night here and we could head north first thing Sunday morning for the day. What do you say to that?'

'Sounds wonderful,' she agreed whilst privately worrying that it sounded like she was becoming more like a girlfriend than a mistress. Dinner out somewhere special. Sleeping over afterwards—not that that was new—and then all day Sunday together. Still, as long as they kept their relationship secret then she supposed it didn't matter how much time they spent together. It was important to Vivienne, keeping their sexual relationship a secret. She didn't want people to think she was a fool, jumping from the frying pan into the fire. After all, Jack was never going to marry her. He'd made that clear up front. Still, if she didn't do something silly like fall in love—again—then there was no reason to worry that she might get burnt by him.

'Good,' Jack said in a satisfied tone. 'Now, I think it's time for seconds...'

CHAPTER SEVENTEEN

'IT'S NOT LIKE you to visit on a Saturday,' Jack's mother said over lunch the following Saturday. He'd rung her the previous night, saying he'd drop in around noon, and she'd told him to stay for lunch.

Jack forked one of the baby beets into his mouth before answering. God, but he did love salads, though he hated making them himself; hated cooking all round. He wondered briefly if Vivienne was a good cook. He imagined she would be. She was good at most things, that girl. Maybe he would ask her to cook him a meal one night, though not in that antiseptic kitchen of hers. Damn, but he wished he could find out why she was so clinical when it came to her own flat's décor.

'Couldn't make it tomorrow,' he explained. 'I'm driving up to Francesco's Folly to see the place again.' He'd told her all about the place during his previous night's phone call. As had become her habit lately, his mother wasn't as surprised as he thought she'd be. In fact, she seemed suspiciously pleased, though that could have been because he'd said she and Jim could go there for romantic weekends once it was finished.

'You'll have to take me up there one day soon,' she suggested.

'I'd rather not till it's refurbished. Actually, I'm not

going alone tomorrow. I'm taking up the designer I've hired to do the interior decorating. She's a girl who's worked for me often, doing my show homes and villas.'

'What's she like, this designer you've hired?'

'What do you mean?'

Eleanor did her best to adopt an ingenuous expression. She knew from past experience that Jack didn't like her questioning him about the women in his life. Something told her—some feminine instinct, or possibly motherly instinct—that this girl might be different. 'Well…er…is she young? Old? Plain? Pretty? The usual questions.'

'I'm not sure how old Vivienne is. Late twenties, I guess. And I'd call her attractive rather than pretty. She does have lovely green eyes, though. And a great figure.'

Aha! So he'd noticed her eyes and her figure. And what a nice name: Vivienne. Classy.

'Single?'

'Yep. Though she was engaged till recently. To some fortune hunter who dumped her for Courtney Ellison. Frank Ellison's daughter, you know? The mining magnate.'

'Yes, I know who you mean. How awful for her, Jack. She must be devastated.'

'She's better off without the likes of him.'

Was that jealousy she heard? Or just dislike? Jack detested men who cheated, and he had a strong sense of responsibility and integrity. He would make some girl a wonderful husband. One day.

'Does Vivienne think that?' she asked quietly.

Jack frowned into his plate. Did she finally? One might have thought so when she was panting beneath him. Or when she lay naked in his arms, satiated from another of their nightly sexathons. But, to be brutally honest, Jack still wasn't sure if Vivienne's wildly wanton act in bed wasn't just that. An act. Not that he thought she was faking her orgasms. Hell, no. No one pretended that noisily.

'Possibly not,' he replied to his mother's question. 'But hopefully she will soon.'

Jack knew as soon as he said 'hopefully' that it was a mistake.

He glanced up to find his mother looking intently at him.

'You like this Vivienne, don't you?'

Jack saw no point in denying it. 'Yep,' he said succinctly, and stabbed a spear of asparagus.

'And does she like you back?' his mother persisted.

'Yep,' he said.

'Are you sleeping with her?'

Jack put down his fork with a sigh. 'Mum. Truly. I'm thirty-seven years old. Who I sleep with is none of your business.'

'You're my son and your relationships will always be my business. It's not as though I'm going to start nagging you to settle down and get married, am I? Though I would if it would work. For what it's worth, I've always thought you'd make some lucky girl a great husband. And you'd be a great father as well, so there!'

Jack rolled his eyes, then went back to eating his salad.

'What if she falls in love with you, Jack? She might, you know. On the rebound.'

Jack scowled. 'Look, she won't fall in love with me, our relationship isn't like that. We're just having fun, no complications and nothing that serious.' Jack said the words, knew they were true, but for some reason he suddenly found himself wishing it were otherwise.

'Oh, Jack, physical intimacy often leads to a deepening of feelings for a woman. It's hard to be intimate with a man and not become emotionally involved. And what if you fall in love with *her*? Have you thought about that?'

Jack practically ground his teeth in exasperation. He should never have told his mum about his relationship with Vivienne. Vivienne was so right: it was best to keep this kind of relationship a secret.

'Don't be silly, Mum. I don't do love.'

She laughed. 'You don't *do* love, Jack. It just happens.'

Jack ignored her.

'I'd like to meet this Vivienne.'

Jack slammed down his fork again. 'Mum, our relationship is not that serious. You don't need to meet her and I don't think she would appreciate it either. Vivienne and I are both completely relaxed about our relationship and there will be no falling in love from either of us!'

Eleanor sighed. He really could be very difficult. Of course, Jack might proclaim that he wasn't falling in love with this Vivienne girl, but perhaps he didn't know that was what was happening to him yet. But it was. She'd heard the jealousy in his voice when he'd been talking about Vivienne's ex. On top of that, this was the first girl he'd ever actually told her about in years. That had to mean something.

'Okay, I'll stop bothering you about her,' she said at last.

'Good,' Jack snapped. 'Now, I'd like to finish my meal, if you don't mind.'

CHAPTER EIGHTEEN

'How did the visit with your mother go yesterday?' Vivienne asked Jack shortly after they took off for the drive up to Nelson's Bay the following morning. 'I forgot to ask you last night.'

In truth, she'd been looking forward to being with him so much by Saturday evening, having not seen him the previous day, that she hadn't been able to focus on anything but how much she wanted him. Dinner out had been a trial and she could hardly remember what she'd eaten or what they'd talked about. It had taken a lot of control for her not to do outrageous things to him during the taxi ride back to Jack's place after dinner—he hadn't taken his car, saying he wanted to have a few drinks—especially after he'd kissed her, slipping a hand up under her skirt at the same time. She'd read about women who went down on men in the back of taxis but had always thought it utterly outrageous. But she'd been tempted. Oh, so tempted.

She shivered as she recalled how close she'd been to coming as Jack had stroked her through her panties. He'd withdrawn his hand—the knowing devil—before she did, leaving her desperate with wanting. She recalled how annoyed she'd felt at how unaffected *he* had seemed at the time. But that had just been pretence on his part. He'd shown her within seconds of closing his apartment door that his desire for her had been just as great. He'd taken her up against that door, not bothering to undress properly.

That he hadn't used a condom only sunk into them both afterwards, Jack profusely apologetic whilst she'd just been shocked, not worried so much. After all, she *was* on the pill. Which she confessed when she saw how upset he was. For the rest of the night, Jack hadn't used protection, assuring her that she was safe from any other kind of health hazard. It had been wonderful not having to bother with protection, not to mention deliciously pleasurable.

Jack glanced across at Vivienne before replying. 'Good,' he said. 'She made my favourite salad for lunch. By the way, I told her about buying Francesco's Folly, and that I'd hired you to do the refurbishment. *And* that I was bringing you up here today to look at the house,' he added, omitting the fact that his mum had asked to meet her.

'Oh? Didn't she think that was odd?'

Jack shot Vivienne a frown. What was it with women that they often jumped to the right conclusions? That mysterious feminine instinct perhaps.

'I don't see why she should. Like I said, I explained the situation. How you've worked for me before. Many times.'

'Maybe so, Jack, but this is Sunday, not a work day.'

Jack shrugged. 'She knows I often work twenty-four-seven. It's nothing new. If you want something to worry about, then how about us going together to that engagement party next Saturday night? The paparazzi are sure to be hanging about and we might get our photos snapped. How are you going to explain that to people if our picture gets in the Sunday gossip columns?'

Vivienne hadn't thought of that. But, once she did, she wasn't overly worried. 'I doubt that will happen. We're not celebrities, Jack. You keep a low public profile and I'm a nobody. They won't be taking pictures of us.'

'Just thought I'd warn you.'

'Fine. I'm warned. Now, can we talk about something else? I don't want to think about next Saturday night. I'm not keen on going but I *am* going, and that's all there is to it. I aim to approach it the same way I do the dentist.'

'What do you mean, the way you approach the dentist?'

'I hate going to the dentist. Silly, really, since the dentist I go to is very gentle. The first time I went to him, though, I hadn't been to the dentist in over ten years. I was so nervous during the days leading up to my appointment that when I got in the chair I almost threw up.

'Anyway, he gave me some gas and a couple of injections and it didn't hurt at all. After that, I started going every six months for check-ups but I still used to feel sick for days beforehand. Finally, I got a grip on myself and decided it was a waste of my nervous energy to worry till I was actually sitting in that chair. I trained myself not to think about it during the days leading up to my next appointment. Though I do allow myself a short burst of nerves when I'm actually in the chair. I'll do the same with that engagement party— I'll think about it when we're walking up the steps of Frank Ellison's mansion.'

'No kidding,' Jack said in a droll tone. 'And I'm the Queen of England.'

Vivienne shrugged. 'Okay, so I might have to give it *some* thought beforehand. I have to buy a dress, for starters. No way am I going to show up looking daggy. Did the invitation say black tie?'

'I think so. Yeah.'

'In that case, it's a tux for you and an evening gown for me. Do you have a tux?'

'I'll get one.'

'You can rent them, you know.'

'I do know that, Vivienne. I'm not a total Philistine. But I always prefer to buy rather than rent. So why did you leave it so long between dental visits?' he asked, finding it strange that such a perfectionist would neglect her teeth like that.

'What? Oh, I…um…that wasn't recently. It was ten years ago, when I was seventeen. After Mum and Dad's divorce, Mum just didn't take me. And I didn't think about it, not till I was in my final year of high school and I got this dreadful toothache.'

'But why didn't she take you? Couldn't she afford to, was that it?'

'No. She had the money. She…she… Oh, it's very complicated, Jack. Please, I don't like talking about those years. I survived and my teeth are fine now. See?' And she flashed an impressive set of pearly whites at him.

Jack only had to look into Vivienne's haunted eyes to know that she might have survived—physically speaking—but she'd been left with some lasting emotional damage. Reading between the lines, he worked out that her mother must have become seriously depressed after the divorce. Divorce was like a death to some women.

He recalled how depressed—and useless—his own mother had been after his father had died and it had taken her years to bounce back. It sounded like Vivienne's mother had never bounced back. Instead, she'd neglected her only child. Very badly, by the sound of things.

Jack would have pried a little more into her background but a quick sidewards glance showed that she'd brought the shutters down, her expression closed and bleak. Jack decided to change the subject.

'We might actually have to do some work up here today, Vivienne,' he said.

She turned happier eyes towards him. 'Oh? What kind of work?'

'Nothing too strenuous. But I want to make up our minds which way to tackle the renovations. Whether we just tart up what's there or go the whole hog and rip out walls.'

'I definitely won't be advising that you rip out any walls, Jack. The floor plan of the house is great. It's just what's *in* the rooms which needs ripping out, especially the bathrooms and kitchens. The bedrooms just need new paint and carpet. And furniture, of course. Plus all those hideous curtains will have to go. Perhaps you could think about double glazing on the windows. And tinted glass, of course. Keep out the glare of the morning sun.'

'Wow. You've really been giving this some thought, haven't you?'

'Well, I had nothing to do all Friday, so I thought I should get started.'

'Good girl.'

'I can't wait to move in. I was thinking next Sunday. Provided you get my contract ready before then, of course,' she added, somewhat cheekily.

'Next Sunday will be fine. And we'll definitely get your contract drawn up and signed this week.'

'Good.'

'Now, you sure you won't find it too lonely up there?'

Vivienne shook her head. 'I'm used to living by myself, Jack,' she said.

Another enigmatic comment. One which he would have liked to explore, but decided not to. Not yet.

'To tell you the truth, I'm looking forward to it,' she added.

In a way, so was Jack. Because he couldn't keep up with what he'd been doing this past week for much longer. He'd found it hard to concentrate on work after making love to Vivienne half the night every night. He was a very hands-on builder and he wasn't as young as he used to be. He'd been glad he had an excuse not to see her on Friday night, giving him the opportunity to recover. Though sleep hadn't come as easily as it did when he was in bed with Vivienne. Sex was a wonderful sleeping tablet, no doubt about that.

But he really did have an important job to complete in the coming weeks, finishing off a block of units, with a killer deadline built into his contract. He couldn't afford to slack off, or let his men slack off. They took the lead from him, he'd found. He knew he wouldn't be able to resist being with Vivienne whilst she was in Sydney but it would be another matter once she was living in Francesco's Folly. He could hardly drop in every evening. He would miss her but it would make the weekends even sweeter. He could just imagine how he would feel by the time he arrived on a Friday evening: more than ready for her to be his beck-and-call girl, that was for sure.

Spots on his windshield brought a frustrated groan. He hated driving in the rain. Especially heavy rain, which was exactly what he was contending with half an hour later. Their usual stop at Raymond Terrace was a respite, but not long enough to last out the rain. It was still pouring when they both ran for the Porsche and dived in.

'I hate this kind of rain,' Jack grumbled. 'Makes a builder's life hell. Puts you behind, big time.'

'You don't have to worry too much about the rain with Francesco's Folly, though,' Vivienne said. 'Most of the work is indoors.'

'True. How long do you think it will take? I'd like it all complete before Christmas.'

'That depends, I guess, on how reliable this builder is you've hired.'

'He's very reliable. And if he isn't, I'll rely on you to crack the whip.'

Vivienne laughed. 'I thought I told you I wasn't that kind of girl.'

'Maybe not in the bedroom, but you're quite formidable at work. Don't forget, I've seen you in action. You always want everything done just so.'

'You ought to talk!'

'We're two peas in a pod, then, aren't we?'

They glanced over at each other, their eyes laughing.

So Jack was surprised when a strange wave of bleak emotion suddenly washed through him. His gaze swung back to the road ahead, his eyebrows bunching together in a frown.

'You do like me now, don't you, Vivienne?' he asked.

His question startled her. Then worried her. Because

it forced her to face the fact that she liked him more and more with each passing day. How long, she wondered, before liking—combined with lust—turned to love? Another week? A month? Six months? Vivienne feared that by the time the refurbishment of Francesco's Folly was complete she would be in much too deep where Jack was concerned. Yet she'd known what she was doing, getting involved with him. He hadn't hidden the fact that he didn't want marriage and children; that he wasn't looking for 'forever' love. Just friendship and fun. He hadn't lied to her. Ever. Which was what she liked about him most of all.

'Very much so,' she said truthfully.

When Jack's heart actually swelled with happiness, his mother's words came back to haunt him.

You don't do love, Jack. It just happens.

Dear God, he thought. But not altogether unhappily. Which was perverse. He'd always believed he didn't want to be bothered with the whole love and marriage scenario, especially the children part. He'd wanted freedom from any more responsibility. But when love struck—as it obviously had—you actually wanted to embrace such things. He could think of nothing more desirable than being married to Vivienne and having children with her. How amazing was that?

Amazing, but also problematic. After all, she didn't love him back, did she?

'That's good,' he said, somewhat distractedly. 'Look, the rain's stopped.' Which was just as well. Jack doubted that Francesco's Folly would look as marvellous in the rain. And he wanted it always to look marvellous. Wanted Vivienne to fall in love with the place, as well as with him. It might take time but that was all right. She wasn't going anywhere fast. She'd be signing that

contract to work for him till the refurbishment was complete. That gave him several months to achieve his goal,
though Jack suspected he would need every single one
of them.

CHAPTER NINETEEN

SHE'D LIED TO Jack about being able to control her nerves over the party. Come the following Saturday morning, she woke with an already churning stomach which quickly worsened once it hit her that D-day had finally arrived: Daryl Day.

She hadn't spent last night at Jack's apartment, because she had an early appointment at the beauty salon just down the road from her own flat. Normally, she enjoyed the couple of hours she spent there every six weeks or so, having her hair trimmed, shampooed and blow-dried, after which she usually had a pedicure and manicure. The owner of the salon, a lady in her early forties, was a bright and breezy conversationalist who made all her clients feel better for their visit to her salon. But nothing was going to make Vivienne feel better that morning.

'What colour do you want on your nails?' the girl asked.

'Red,' Vivienne replied, thinking of the red evening gown which was hanging up on the front of her wardrobe. It was too long to hang inside, and had cost her a bomb. 'A bright, dark red.'

'This one is very popular,' the girl said, holding up a bottle of dark red varnish that had a shimmer in it.

'It's called Scarlet Woman. There's a lipstick to match, if you'd like to buy it.'

Vivienne suspected the girls got a commission if the clients bought some of their products. Usually, she didn't say yes to their offers, preferring to buy her hair-care products and cosmetics online. But this time she said yes to the lipstick. She might not feel confident about tonight, but by golly she was going to look it!

The expression on Jack's face when she opened her door to him at eight that evening was gratifying, even if the butterflies in her stomach had by then reached epic proportions. She was also grateful for the distraction of how fabulous he looked in his black-tie outfit. Not just tall, dark and handsome, but very sophisticated.

'Heavens, Jack!' she exclaimed before he could say a word about her. 'You do scrub up well. And that tux is amazing. It looks like it was made for you.' Which it did, fitting his broad-shouldered physique to perfection with not a wrinkle anywhere. She'd half- imagined he might look out of place in formal clothes but she was wrong.

He smiled. 'It was, actually. I couldn't find anything off the peg to fit me so I had no alternative. And might I say the same about your outfit? Red suits you.'

Strangely, it wasn't a colour she'd worn before. She'd always thought it too in-your-face. But in-your-face was the look she was going for tonight, the red having extra impact because the material had a glitter effect, similar to her lipstick and nail varnish. The style of the dress was not her usual style either, being *very* tight. And, whilst it had long sleeves and a high neckline, the back was cut very low, along with a split in the back seam from the hem up to her knees—possibly put there so the occupant of the dress could actually walk.

'You look like you've stepped out of one of those glamorous movies they used to make in the old days,' Jack said. 'Especially with your hair done that way.'

Vivienne's hand lifted to pat the jewelled comb which anchored one side of her hair back from her face, the other side waving down over her shoulder in the way, yes, the movie stars of the forties used to do their hair.

'You really like it?' she said, her voice a wee bit tremulous. Those butterflies were acting up again.

'What's not to like?' Jack replied. 'You look good enough to eat and you know it, so don't come that coy nonsense with me. If ever a look was designed to make an ex-fiancé feel regret and his new fiancée feel jealous, then you've nailed it tonight. I just hope you won't regret it yourself.'

'Why should I?' Vivienne shot back with a surge of sudden defiance. 'I've done nothing to regret.'

'Not yet. But just remember if you fire bullets at people they just might fire some back. But it's too late now. Cinderella is going to the ball.'

Vivienne rolled her eyes. 'I can't see Cinderella wearing a dress like this, can you?'

'Not quite,' he said, and eyed her up and down with a decidedly sexual gaze.

'In that case we're well matched, because you're far from Prince Charming,' she threw back at him. 'Come on, let's get going. The sooner we get there and I say what I have to say, the sooner we can leave.' *And the sooner those butterflies will stop their infernal wing flapping!*

Jack didn't say another word till they were on their

way. Fortunately, when he did speak, it wasn't about tonight.

'Are you all packed and ready for the big move north tomorrow?' he asked.

'Of course,' she replied. 'I'm a very organised person. Everything's already in the boot of my car.'

'I'll drive over to your place in my car around nine and you can follow me up in yours.'

'All right. Do you have the keys to the house?'

'Not yet. We'll have to pick them up on the way. I've also organized for the builder to drop by around one, so that you can meet him. His name's Ken. Ken Struthers.'

'Fine.'

'Are Daryl's folks going to be there tonight?'

Vivienne was taken aback by this abrupt change of topic. 'What? No, no, he's estranged from his family.'

'How come that doesn't surprise me?'

'He said they weren't very nice people. He was put into a foster home when he was only ten.'

'And you believed him?'

That brought Vivienne up short. She sighed. 'Yes, I did at the time. More fool me. But don't worry, that fool has been well and truly put to bed. Daryl could tell me the world was round now and I wouldn't believe him. I despise the man and I aim to tell him so. Like you said, Jack, tonight is all about closure.'

Jack glanced over at Vivienne just as her red-glossed lips pressed hard together in a determined pout.

Oh dear, he thought. It was going to be a difficult night.

CHAPTER TWENTY

SECURITY AT THE Ellison mansion was tight; Jack had to be checked off at the gates as a guest on the guard's list. He even had to show the guy his driver's licence, which rather underlined Vivienne's statement that neither of them had easy-to-recognise celebrity status. There weren't paparazzi obviously lurking about the gate; there was a helicopter hovering which might have been filled with photographers, but more likely more security. Frank Ellison was paranoid when it came to protecting his patch and his privacy.

As he was directed to one of the multitude of parking spaces available in the huge grounds, Jack experienced a measure of pride at how magnificent the house looked at night, lit up by the literally thousands of lights Frank had commissioned him to build in everywhere: the façade, the roof, the garden, not to mention each of the two-dozen stone steps which led up to the impressive entrance.

'Is this the biggest house you've ever built?' Vivienne asked him as he guided her carefully up the steps, his hand on her left elbow.

'By far,' he replied. 'I presume this is the biggest house you've decorated as well.'

'Absolutely. It took me over six months, even with lots of help.'

'Building the house took two years.'

'I can imagine. I hope you made plenty of money out of it.'

He grinned over at her. 'Heaps.'

'Good,' she said, and there was that determined look again.

Once they reached the massive front porch, with only the equally massive front doors separating them from the party inside—you could hear the music from outside—Vivienne sucked in sharply and squared her shoulders.

'It's not too late to change your mind,' Jack said quietly by her side, even as he reached to ring the doorbell.

But it was already too late; both doors flung open before his finger connected with the buzzer.

And there stood Frank Ellison, as huge as his house. Around sixty, he had a large, florid face, and an even larger stomach.

'I told them to keep these damned things open,' he boomed before noticing his new arrivals. 'Jack! You came. I'm so glad you did. And who's this stunning creature by your side?'

He hadn't recognised Vivienne, Jack realised. Of course, she did look different from how she did in her work wardrobe.

But still...

Vivienne thought it was typical of the man that he didn't recognise her. He'd rarely spoken to her during the months she'd worked on this house. They'd only ever had one decent conversation when he'd actually looked at her, and that was the day he'd come to Classic Design to hire their services.

'Money's no object,' he'd said. 'Just make sure everyone else knows that. I want the place to look like it's owned by royalty. Or a filthy-rich sheikh. You got that, girlie?'

She'd got it. And she'd delivered. The place was seriously palatial, from the Italian marble floors to the exquisite furniture—all genuine antiques—the air of opulence enhanced by the seriously expensive artwork hanging on every single wall.

'It's Vivienne, Mr Ellison,' she said with a cool smile. 'Vivienne Swan. I was the interior decorator for this house. Don't you remember me?'

He didn't look embarrassed in the slightest. 'Yes, of course I remember you. I just didn't recognise you in that smashing red dress. So, you and Jack are dating, are you? I didn't realise that when he told me you were the best interior decorator in Sydney. A somewhat biased recommendation, eh, Jack?' he said, with a 'nod nod, wink wink' grin. 'Not that you didn't do a fabulous job, girlie. Actually, both of you did a fabulous job. I couldn't be happier with the finished product. Couldn't be happier tonight all round, with my daughter finally finding herself a bloke man enough to put a bun in her oven. And then to actually agree to marry her!'

Vivienne realised in that instant that Frank Ellison had no idea she'd once been engaged to his daughter's fiancé. He obviously didn't recall her being with Daryl at their house-warming party. He'd probably been too busy impressing his other celebrity guests that night to notice her, or who she was with.

Which was fine by her. She hadn't come here to have a go at Frank Ellison.

The arrival of other guests at that moment had Frank

telling Jack and Vivienne to go inside and mingle whilst he turned his attention elsewhere.

'He doesn't know you were engaged to Daryl,' Jack muttered to her as they walked under the huge chandelier which hung from the ceiling of the massive marble-floored atrium.

'No,' she agreed. 'Maybe Courtney doesn't know, either. Come to think of it, I wasn't wearing an engagement ring when we came to Frank's house-warming party. Daryl had asked me to marry him but I...er... he...um...hadn't bought the ring yet.' No way was she going to admit in front of Jack that she'd eventually bought her own engagement ring. That would be just too humiliating for words. 'She probably only knows what Daryl told her, which would be a pack of lies.'

Jack's laugh was dry. 'Courtney knew about you, Vivienne. I'd put my money on it.'

As if on cue, the girl herself, resplendent in a cocktail dress which made Vivienne's gown look demure, came undulating up the three steps which separated the foyer from the huge sunken living room. Her dress—obviously a one-off made for her—was black and strapless, the beaded bodice cut so low across and between Courtney's impressive and possibly enhanced breasts that it only just covered her nipples. The skirt was black chiffon, flaring out from just under her bust, effectively hiding her baby bump, and ending with a handkerchief hemline which flowed around the girl's ankles, their slender shape shown off by the highest, slinkiest, sparkliest shoes Vivienne had ever seen. Even more sparkly were the exquisite diamond earrings hanging from Courtney's lobes.

Much as she tried, she could not fault the girl's face, with its perfect skin, cutely turned-up nose and pouty mouth, though Vivienne did wonder how much was natural and how much was owed to the skills of a top plastic surgeon. After all, her father wasn't even remotely handsome, so she hadn't got any beauty genes from him. Obviously they came from her mother, whoever she was. Frank Ellison had had lots of wives, and they'd all been good-looking. Men like that didn't marry plain women. Even so, Courtney's long mane of creamy blonde hair definitely wasn't real—those dark roots were a dead giveaway—though it did suit her. One could not deny that Courtney Ellison was a very sexy creature all round; Vivienne's admiration for Jack went up a few notches at his having resisted her advances.

Daryl trailed several paces after his fiancée, sipping a glass of champagne, not having noticed Vivienne as yet. He was looking back over his shoulder at a striking brunette who was smiling invitingly after him. Leopards didn't change their spots, Vivienne realised ruefully as her gaze swung from the brunette back to her ex.

There was no doubt Daryl was elegantly handsome in his black dinner suit and bow tie, but not nearly as impressive as Jack. As he made his way slowly across the expansive lobby, Vivienne began to see the weakness in Daryl's features, and foppishness in his walk. She even found new criticism in the way he wore his hair, the streaked blond locks flopping onto his forehead in a style way too young for a man in his thirties.

It pleased Vivienne that she no longer felt one ounce of unhappiness, or jealousy, or envy, over the situation. If anything, she felt a little sorry for Courtney, having Daryl's baby. He would make a horrible father.

'Jack!' Courtney gushed, and reached up to give him a slightly too-long kiss on the cheek, at the same time throwing Vivienne a sharp glance, as though trying to place her. 'How lovely to see you again. Thank you so much for coming. And thank you for the lovely present you sent.'

Vivienne's eyebrows arched. He'd sent them a present?

'My mother always says a girl can't have too many irons,' Jack said with a brilliantly straight face whilst Vivienne suppressed a gasp. He'd sent her an *iron*, this billionaire's daughter who'd never ironed a thing in her life?

Courtney looked startled, betraying that she'd had no idea what he'd actually sent. There were probably myriad unwrapped presents piled high in one of the myriad bedrooms.

Daryl finally caught up with his fiancée, only to see his *ex*-fiancée standing in front of him.

'My God!' he exclaimed, his voice thin and high. 'Vivienne!'

Courtney's blonde head jerked back as she stared at Vivienne, then Daryl, then Jack.

'Is this some kind of cruel joke?' she demanded to know, her porcelain-like cheeks flushing with anger.

'Not at all, Courtney,' Jack replied as smooth as silk. 'Daryl's moved on, and so has Vivienne. She and I have become…good friends. There's no hard feelings over your stealing her fiancé, are there, Vivienne?'

'None at all, darling,' she replied, glad when Jack didn't bat an eyelid at her endearment. She'd decided on the spur of the moment not to bother tearing verbal strips off Daryl. Just being here with Jack by her side was the best revenge. She could see Daryl was shocked, and most put out. And so was Courtney, which meant she'd known about her all along. She might not have recognised her, the same way her self-absorbed and self-centred father hadn't recognised her. But she had known. Suddenly, Vivienne didn't feel sorry for her at all. She was getting what she deserved: Daryl as a husband, with all his vanity, greed and selfishness.

'You did me a good turn, Courtney,' Vivienne added with a brilliant smile as she touched Jack tenderly on the arm.

Courtney's blue eyes darkened appreciably. 'Really,' she bit out.

Her father joining them rather stopped any further conversation on the subject.

'Don't stand around in the foyer, folks,' Frank said expansively. 'Let's go down to where all the food and wine are being served. I would be totally miffed if you didn't taste some of the specialities I ordered in, Jack. And you too, Vivienne. Caviar from Russia and truffles from France, not to mention several cases of their best champagne. Nothing like champagne.'

The next half hour went quite well—which meant without anyone creating a scene—with a none-the-wiser Frank plying Jack and Vivienne with champagne and caviar, whilst Courtney eventually took Daryl off somewhere, hopefully to have a lover's spat. Vivienne wasn't blind. She could see that Courtney was totally miffed. Vivienne was glad that she'd gone to so much trouble with her appearance. She knew she looked good.

Frank finally left them alone and they wandered out onto the massive back terrace, Vivienne happy not to have to make further chitchat with the kind of people Frank courted: all rich snobs who thought they were better than everyone else, just because they could afford habourside mansions and more than one Picasso.

'So I'm darling now, am I?' were Jack's first words as they strolled alongside the well-lit, Olympic-sized pool. There was no one else around. A pool party, it was not, though there were several portable heaters dotted around for warmth.

'Sorry. I couldn't resist. I thought it was a better revenge, his believing I'd moved on almost as quickly as he had. You didn't mind, did you?'

Of course I minded, Jack thought. But it was impossible to say so. Stupid, too. 'Not at all,' he lied. 'I thought you conducted yourself brilliantly. Much better than you saying things you might regret. Dignity is always the best policy.'

'I thought honesty was the best policy.'

'That too.'

'In that case, I want to tell you how much I appreciate having you by my side tonight, Jack. I can honestly say you are more of a man than Daryl could ever be.'

Jack's heart lurched in his chest. Hopefully, it didn't show on his face how much her compliment meant to him. Because, despite her voicing admiration for him, he knew that Vivienne still wasn't ready yet to fall in love again.

'That's sweet of you to say so…darling,' he added with a cheeky smile, determined to keep a light note to the evening. 'I presume you don't want to leave yet?'

'I don't think we should,' Vivienne answered, despite really wanting to. 'Frank might be offended, and he's not a man you should offend. I don't care for myself but he'd be a dangerous enemy for you to have, Jack.'

'I don't give a damn about Ellison. I'll survive without his patronage. But if you like we'll stay a while and stick it to Daryl some more.'

'Good idea. Now, I simply *have* to go to the ladies'. All this champagne. Wait for me here, would you?'

Handing Jack her now empty glass, she turned and made her way slowly back inside.

Jack watched her go, thinking how classy she was. The kind of woman a man would be lucky to marry.

He sighed, then wandered over to the nearest out-door setting where he put down the two champagne glasses. He was about to turn and walk back towards the house—he'd made up his mind to collect Vivienne and leave—when he saw Daryl slink out of the pool house, hurriedly doing up his trousers. A sexy-looking brunette followed, giggling and sorting out her own dishevelled clothes. When Daryl saw Jack watching them, he said something to the brunette, who hurried off whilst Daryl sauntered over to Jack with a smarmy guilt lurking in his heavy-lidded eyes.

'It's not what you think,' came the cliché.

'Why should you care *what* I think?' Jack returned coldly.

'I don't. I just don't want you to make trouble for me and Courtney.'

'I don't give a damn what you do, mate. Just keep away from Vivienne.'

Daryl laughed. 'I won't be going back there, mate. Trust me on that. She's too screwed up for me. Not only a tidy nut but bloody boring in bed. Lord knows what you see in her. Great body, though. I'll give her that.'

Jack gritted his teeth. Hard. There was only so much a man in love could take. His right fist shot out before he could stop it, connecting with Daryl's decidedly soft stomach with the force of a jackhammer. Daryl made a whooshing sound as he doubled over, all the air rushing from his lungs like a pricked balloon. And then he did something even better than collapsing at Jack's feet. Clutching his stomach, he stupidly tried to straighten up, staggering backwards to the edge of the pool before falling, arms flailing widely, into the water.

He didn't scream, thank goodness; he possibly didn't have enough air left in his lungs. Though he did manage some spluttered expletives once he resurfaced, by which time Vivienne had returned from her trip to the toilet.

'What happened?' she asked Jack on sighting Daryl floundering in the water. 'Is he drunk or what?'

'He hit me!' Daryl spluttered.

'He deserved it,' Jack replied coolly.

Daryl finally made it over to the side of the pool. 'I'll get you,' he threatened. 'I'll tell Frank you assaulted me and he'll ruin you.'

Jack immediately strode over and bent down to grab one of Daryl's hands, crunching his fingers painfully whilst whispering in his ear at the same time. 'You say a single word and I'll tell Courtney all about the brunette I saw you with in the pool house just now.'

That shut him up, especially when Courtney herself made an appearance, also wanting to know what had happened.

'Just an accident, babe,' a sodden Daryl said after Jack hauled him out of the water. 'I bent down to wash my hands and overbalanced. No great drama.'

'But you've ruined your nice new suit!' she wailed.

'For Pete's sake,' he threw back at her, his temper obviously fraying. 'It's just a suit.'

Jack could see the beginning of a nice little argument there. Which was almost as satisfying as hitting the bastard.

'Come on, Vivienne,' he said, and took her arm. 'Let's go home.'

'What did you mean by he deserved it?' she whispered as Jack steered her swiftly back inside the house, across the living room and up the steps to the foyer. 'What did he say to you to make you hit him?'

'Later, Vivienne,' he told her, not sure what reason he would give. Because what Daryl had said would hurt Vivienne and Jack didn't want to do that. Okay, yes, she was excessively tidy, but to call her screwed up was insulting. As for her being boring in bed... What planet was Daryl from to call her that? Vivienne was anything but boring in bed. It was all decidedly odd.

Fortunately, Vivienne held her tongue till they were in the car and safely away. But he should have known that female curiosity would soon get the better of her.

'I can't wait any longer, Jack,' she said when he pulled up at a set of lights. 'I'm dying to know what happened between the two of you. And I want the truth, the whole truth and nothing but the truth.'

Jack winced. 'Are you sure about that, Vivienne?'

'Positive. Look, I just want to know what he said to make you hit him. I've been thinking, and I presume it was something bad about me.'

'Not that bad,' he said.

'But not too complimentary. Out with it, Jack. No lies now. And no watering down. Give it to me straight.'

'Okay,' Jack agreed, seeing that it really was the only way. On the plus side, he could then ask her some questions he'd always wanted to ask. 'He said you were a tidy nut and boring in bed.' He decided to leave out the 'screwed up' part.

He glanced across in time to see her blush fiercely.

'I see,' she said stiffly. 'Well, I guess he was only telling the truth.'

'Don't be ridiculous,' Jack snapped. 'Okay, so you are a bit uptight when it comes to clutter, but that's hardly a crime. As for being boring in bed... Well, you and I both know that's a bald-faced lie,' he added, trying to bring a smile to her face.

It didn't.

The lights went green and Jack roared off, upset that the evening looked like it was ending badly.

'I'm not going to let you go all quiet on me, Vivienne,' he said firmly when she just sat there in silence. 'I want to know why Daryl said you were boring in bed. Because it doesn't make any damned sense to me.'

CHAPTER TWENTY-ONE

VIVIENNE KNEW BY the look on Jack's face that nothing less than the truth would satisfy him. Which was fair enough, she supposed. She just hoped he wouldn't jump to conclusions over why she'd been different with him sexually. She didn't want him to think that it was because she'd been falling in love with him, or that this process had probably started long before she was aware of it. For how could you not fall in love with a man who'd come to your rescue with flowers and a fascinating job when you needed it most? A man who'd saved your life and held you close, then made love to you endlessly with a passion which had been as healing as it had been wonderful?

But the coup de grâce was the way Jack had stood up for her tonight. Oh…the satisfaction she'd felt when she'd discovered he'd flattened Daryl, and then when he'd said 'he deserved it'.

Jack was her hero, her knight in shining armour. The man she loved. Truly, really loved. What she'd felt for Daryl had been nothing more than a mirage.

But she could not tell Jack that. If she did, he would run a mile. And she couldn't bear that. He might never love her back but she could not voluntarily do anything to lose him. So she would tell him other things. Not lies, exactly, but not the total truth.

'Could this wait till I get home and out of this dress?' she said.

He frowned. 'This isn't some kind of procrastinating ploy, is it, Vivienne? Because I aim to get some answers. Don't go thinking you can avoid it by seducing me.'

Vivienne blinked. Now *there* was a thought! Not the right one, however.

'Don't be silly,' she said. 'I'm just uncomfortable, that's all. This dress is dreadfully tight.'

Jack knew she was stalling but he didn't say anything further, just drove her home and helped her out of the car and inside, where she fairly bolted for the bedroom, telling him she wouldn't be long.

He sat down on the black leather sofa, his determination to get answers deepening with the time she took to emerge. When she finally did, she was wrapped in the same fluffy white dressing gown and slippers that she'd worn on that fateful day he'd come here to hire her less than two weeks ago. He suspected she wasn't wearing anything underneath this time, either. Or not very much. She'd taken the jewelled comb out of her hair, he noted, and spread her hair out onto her shoulders in sexy disarray. As much as she looked good enough to eat, he resolved not to be swayed or distracted from getting those answers he wanted.

'You want coffee?' she asked.

'I wouldn't mind,' he said, standing up and following her out to the kitchen which was as clean and clutter free as always. Seeing her place again—he hadn't been inside there lately—underlined the fact that her tidiness *did* verge on obsessive.

'I still don't have much food to offer you,' she said,

and turned from the kettle to give him a small, some-what wry smile. 'Someone's been taking me out to din-ner every night.'

'Lucky you. But I don't want any food, Vivienne. What I want is for us to talk.'

Vivienne sucked in a deep breath, letting it out slowly as she turned and carried the two mugs of black coffee over to where Jack was already sitting at the kitchen table.

'First things first,' he said. 'Let's go back to Daryl's "boring in bed" accusation. I'm presuming, from what you said, that you weren't the same with him that you are with me. Is that right?'

'Well...um...yes,' she admitted with a small shud-der. 'If you must know, I haven't done most of what I've done with you with him.'

Jack's male ego might have been flattered if he didn't still worry she might have been indulging in some kind of crazy act with him, brought on by Daryl dumping her. 'Why was that, do you think? Were you just pre-tending to be sexy? Acting out some role with me?'

There was no doubting her shock. 'No! I never acted with you, Jack. Never. I loved everything I did with you. I...I'm not sure why I'm so different with you. I just was, right from the start. You made me feel things that Daryl never did. I still don't quite understand it myself. I just know that I love having sex with you and I wouldn't give it up for the world.'

Jack liked the sound of that. 'We do have great chem-istry together,' he said. 'Now, whilst we're having an honest chat, do you think you might tell me why your place looks like it does? I don't mean the tidiness part so much. I'm talking about the starkness of the décor. Because let's face it, Vivienne, it's just not you.'

Vivienne's first instinct was to clam up about that. But then she realised that, if she couldn't tell the man she loved, who could she tell?

Still, it wasn't going to be easy. Not that she thought Jack would be judgemental: he'd had some experience with emotionally fragile mothers so he would understand better than most.

She sighed. 'I will have to go way back to the years before my dad left us…'

'I'm listening,' Jack said gently. He could sense her reluctance but wasn't about to let her off the hook.

She looked at him for a long moment before going on. 'Have you ever watched that show on TV about hoarders?'

'I have, actually. Once or twice.' Jack was about to add that he'd been totally disgusted and revolted by the state of some of the houses those people lived in when he stopped himself short.

Vivienne sighed again. 'I can see by the look on your face that the penny has dropped. Yes, my mother was a hoarder.'

Jack wasn't shocked so much as sad. For Vivienne. What kind of childhood would she have had if she'd been forced to grow up in the kind of filthy place he'd seen on that show?

'I see,' he said. And he did. He could imagine that the children of hoarders would either grow up like them or become diametrically opposite. It certainly explained why Vivienne had an obsession with cleanliness and clutter in her own home.

'So is that why your father left in the first place?' he asked.

'Yes. He couldn't bear it any more.'

'Was she always a hoarder?'

'No, not at all. I remember when I was little, Mum always kept the house beautifully. But after my baby brother died—he was only a week old—she became very depressed. Some days she couldn't even get out of bed.'

'Didn't your father take her to a doctor?'

'She wouldn't go.'

Jack nodded. 'So that's when the hoarding started?' he asked.

'Yes. Not only wouldn't she get rid of all the things she'd bought for the baby but she started buying more: clothes. Furniture. Toys. Like Brendan was still alive. We could have outfitted half the babies in Australia with what she bought. She used to go shopping every day, till one day she suddenly refused to leave the house. After that, she discovered online shopping.'

'So your house wasn't dirty, just full of baby clothes?'

'It was dirty too. Impossible to clean rooms when they're full of stuff. There wasn't a room in the house— or a surface anywhere—which was free of things. The kitchen too. Even the sink. In the end, we lived on take-away. The delivered kind.'

'So that's all you ate? Pizzas and rubbish like that?'

'Yes. For a long while. But when I started high school and realised I was getting fat, I put my foot down and demanded healthier food. But Mum wasn't interested in cooking and the kitchen was a disaster area. I tried cleaning it up when I came home from school but the job became overwhelming.

'In the end, I negotiated moving into the master bed-room which had an *en suite* and enough room for me to set up my own small kitchen. Just a microwave and toaster, really, and a small bar fridge which Dad had left behind in his den. I got Mum to give me an allowance from the money Dad sent so that I could buy my own food and clothes. When I was home, I lived in just that room and let the rest of the house go to pot. Of course, I couldn't have any friends over for sleepovers, so I didn't have any close girlfriends till I left school and moved out. No boyfriends, either, of course. By then, I wasn't large on social skills where the opposite sex is concerned. I was a virgin till I was twenty-one, which I dare say is some kind of record these days.'

'I would say it is for someone as beautiful as you. Which you are, Vivienne, inside and out. And brave too. That is a terribly sad story. But you survived, and for that I have nothing but admiration for you. So how long ago was it that your mother had her heart attack?'

Vivienne grimaced. 'She didn't actually have a heart attack. She tripped over the stuff she'd piled up on the stairs, fell down and broke her neck. I warned her that she'd have an accident in the house one day but she wouldn't listen. Of course, after I moved out, things got much worse. The stairs were chock-a-block with things. Not just baby things now, other stuff she didn't need: shoes. Handbags. Lamps. Ornaments. Silly things. When she didn't answer the phone one evening—I used to ring her every night—I came over and found her body at the foot of the stairs.'

'Oh, Vivienne. That must have been dreadful for you.'

'It was,' she choked out, the memory still having the power to upset her. She'd loved her mother, despite everything. Not that she'd ever felt loved in return. Maybe that was why she'd been so susceptible to Daryl. Because he'd told her he loved her all the time; had even made her believe it. That was what had devastated her the most, to find out his declarations of love had been nothing but a lie, right from the start. At least Jack didn't lie to her. She respected that. When she glanced up and saw the concerned look on his face, she smiled a small, sad smile.

'It's all right, Jack,' she said. 'I'm not going to cry. Frankly, in a way, Mum's dying was a relief. Let's face it, she'd been wretchedly unhappy for years and years. I'm surprised she hadn't committed suicide before that. She often threatened it. Anyway, after the funeral I hired a rubbish removal company to clear the house out, then I hired industrial cleaners to clean it from top to bottom. I couldn't bear to do anything in there. It hurt too much to even look at it. Once it was fit to sell, I auctioned it off. I wanted it gone and I didn't care what price I got for it.

'Strangely enough, it sold for an amazingly good price. The agent explained that, despite its slightly dilapidated state, the house was in a prime location and the block of land was large. I got enough money to buy this place and have it totally renovated, with enough left over to attract the likes of Daryl. Till he met someone seriously rich, of course,' she added.

Jack's fingers tightened around the handle of his coffee mug when he heard the bitterness in her voice. How long would it be before she got over that creep? He felt reasonably confident she no longer loved Daryl, but that kind of betrayal was hard to forget and impossible to forgive. It also made a person reluctant to trust.

Patience, Jack, he lectured himself. *Patience.*

'Like I've already told you several times, Vivienne: you're better off without the likes of him. You're still a young woman. You have your whole life ahead of you.' *With me,* he was dying to say but couldn't. Not yet. 'Plenty of time to get married and have children, if that's what you want. Meanwhile, you can afford to be selfish for a while. Do things that give you pleasure. Live for the moment. You're looking forward to making over Francesco's Folly, aren't you?'

Her bleak eyes actually lit up. 'Oh yes.'

'Though, I must insist, I want the decorator I usually have and not the one who did *this* place, thank you very much,' he said bluntly.

She laughed. 'Fair enough.'

'And just think, on top of the pleasure and satisfaction you'll get from doing a brilliant job, you'll have *me* all to yourself every weekend. That can't be too bad, since you like having sex with me so much. And, let's face it, I'm going to be randy as hell after not seeing you all week. You won't be able to keep up with me.'

Vivienne smiled. 'You should know better than to challenge me, boss. I am competitive by nature. And obsessive to boot. I can guarantee you'll be the one to cry for mercy before I do.'

'I have only one thing to say to that, missy.'

'What's that?'

'Bring it on.'

CHAPTER TWENTY-TWO

VIVIENNE WANDERED THROUGH the upstairs apartment, turning on all the lights—it got dark early in the winter—and checking that everything was just so. She'd decided on finishing this area of Francesco's Folly first whilst she lived in one of the downstairs apartments. It was the easiest part to change, but it had still taken close to two months to complete, mainly because some of the furniture she'd ordered had taken six weeks to arrive. But she was extremely happy with the results and she thought Jack would be too.

She hadn't let him see any of it yet, teasing him that it was all black and white and horribly minimalist, with nothing but black leather, glass furniture and fake Picassos on the walls.

Vivienne could not wait for Jack to arrive tonight, because tonight was the big reveal. She felt as excited as a kid on Christmas morning, glancing at her watch as she hurried downstairs and along past the pool to the balcony which was closest to the driveway. It was nearly six. He would be here soon; he usually left Sydney around three. Friday afternoon traffic was tricky, though. He sometimes got held up getting out of the city, or on the motorway. But if that was the case he would ring her and let her know he was running late, and she'd received no such call this afternoon.

He was very considerate that way. He also brought her the most gorgeous bunch of red roses every Friday, which she found so sweet. It made her hope that his feelings for her were gradually becoming as strong as her feelings for him. Then, one day, he might decide he didn't want to stay a bachelor for ever; that marriage and children and a life here at Francesco's Folly was what he wanted after all.

But she didn't let her hopes get too high. Jack was still very passionate with her. Their weekends together were wonderful, but a few times lately she had caught him falling oddly silent and looking off into the distance. They would often sit and share a bottle of wine on the balcony on a Saturday afternoon. Last weekend, when she had asked him what he was thinking about, he'd said nothing much. Just life. It was an odd answer for him. Odd for him to sit and think like that. He wasn't overly keen on thinking.

Vivienne could not help but worry that he might break off their relationship once Francesco's Folly was finished. It was a depressing thought, but one which she refused to entertain too often. For now, she was happy. Or as happy as a girl could be under the circumstances. Still, she was careful not to do or say anything which might spoil the rest of their time together. She never told him that she loved him, even when the words were in danger of tripping off the end of her tongue—especially when he was making love to her. She always bit her tongue and said something else. Or nothing at all.

Her heart lifted as it always did when she saw headlights turn into the driveway at the bottom of the hill. Jack was home. Safely home.

Whirling, she ran inside so that she could be there, waiting for him when he came in. She didn't run all the way to the front door. That would have been too needy. Too clingy. She went to the kitchen, ostensibly to check that the curry she was making was fine. Which, of course, it was. She always cooked for him on a Friday night, knowing he would be too tired after his long drive to take her out anywhere. Besides, she liked to conserve his energy for other things.

'Honey, I'm home,' he called out as he walked in, one arm full of red roses as usual. And a bottle of champagne in the other.

'Is this to celebrate the big reveal?' she said, beaming.

For a split second, he hesitated to answer. And then he bent to give her a brief peck on the lips. 'But of course. What else?'

Why, she wondered, did his voice sound so odd, as though he was disappointed about something? Had she said something wrong? Done something wrong?

'I made your favourite curry,' she raced on as she put the bottle of champagne in the fridge. When she turned, she found him arranging the roses in the vase which was always at the ready on the pine counter. 'You know you don't have to buy me flowers *every* week.'

'But I like to,' he said, and smiled at her. 'Come on, best show me Francesco's apartment before we do anything else. I know that's what you want to do. You've been talking about nothing else every night this week. But be warned, if I don't like it, you're in big trouble.'

'Oh dear,' she said with mock worry, because she was sure he was going to like it.

He did. In fact, he *loved* it, even the fact that she had had all the walls stripped back and painted white. Not a

stark white, however; a soft off-white which had a hint
of cream in it. It was the perfect backdrop for the furniture she'd chosen: Mediterranean style pieces made
of richly grained wood, which gave the place the kind
of solid but warm feel she'd seen in pictures of Tuscan
villas she'd sourced on the Internet. The deep plump
sofas and chairs she'd chosen for the living room were
covered in soft linens in warm colours: creams, fawns
and a buttery yellow, with the occasional splash of olive-
green thrown in. The fireplace remained, its once-heavy
wooden surround replaced by Italian marble made in a
warm brown shot with gold streaks.

The two *en suite* bathrooms and kitchen were white,
of course, but she'd used the same brown marble on
the counter tops and dual vanities. The fittings were
gold—though not real gold—evoking quality without
being over the top. The living areas were tiled in large
cream tiles, with thick rugs dotted here and there for
warmth and colour. The carpets in the bedrooms were
sable, which went well with everything.

What pleased Jack the most—and consequently
thrilled Vivienne—was her choice of artwork, both
for the walls inside the apartment and the art gallery
on the top landing. Not originals and not worth a fortune, either: prints of famous landscapes and seascapes,
which definitely looked like things he would recognise:
beautiful beaches and graceful sailing boats. Stately
mountains and picturesque valleys. Their frames were
expensive, however. Some were gilt, some shabby-chic
white, depending on where they were positioned.

'You like, boss?' she said cheekily when he just stood
staring at one seascape for a long time. It was hanging
over the fireplace in the living room, and was of a spectacular beach on a rugged coastline.

'Too much,' he replied.

'How can you like anything too much?' It was a peculiar thing to say.

He didn't answer her, just turned away from the picture abruptly and strode across to the sliding glass doors which led out onto the balcony. He reefed one back and stepped out into the cold night air, going over to where the rusted and broken railing had been replaced by clear panels of toughened glass. Vivienne followed him out there, unsure what was happening here. He stood at the railing for a long time in silence before turning and facing a by-then shivering Vivienne. Inside was air-conditioned, but outside was now very chilly.

'I'm sorry,' he said abruptly. 'I thought I could do this but I can't. Not any longer.'

'Do what?' Vivienne asked, suddenly feeling sick to the stomach.

'Wait…till Francesco's Folly is finished.'

So this was it, she thought despairingly. He was going to break it off with her.

She wanted to scream that she wasn't ready yet. That she needed longer with him.

But then she realised that no amount of time would ever be enough. If he didn't care about her the way she cared about him, then what was the point of delaying things?

'So what is it you're trying to say, Jack?' she said, desperately trying to hide her wretchedness. 'You don't want me any more? Is that it?'

His eyes widened, his head jerking back. 'Good God, woman, nothing could be further from the truth. Not *want* you any more? I want you every minute of every day. I love you, Vivienne, so much that not being able to say the words is slowly killing me. I can't play this game any more. I thought I could wait till you fell in love with me before I said anything but I find I can't. Seeing this place tonight...this absolutely glorious place...I don't want to ever live here by myself. I want to live here with you. As husband and wife.'

'Husband and wife?' she choked out.

Jack could see that he'd shocked her but nothing was going to stop him now that he'd opened his mouth and said something. 'Yes, I know I said I didn't want to get married and have children,' he raved on. 'But that was before I fell in love with you, Vivienne. Love changes things. It makes you want more. And, yes, I know it's probably still too soon for you. But do you think you might possibly come to love me one day? You already like me, I know, and you like having sex with me, so loving me is not such a big leap.

'I promise you that, if you marry me, I will do everything in my power to make you happy. I will never cheat on you. Never. And I'll give you anything you want. You can have a hundred children, if that's what you want. No, wait...perhaps not that many...but two or three, or even four, I would consider. Three is not a good number. Yes, four would be good. So what do you say, my darling, beautiful Vivienne? Would you at least think about it?'

She didn't say a single word. She just stared at him, then burst into tears.

Oh God, Jack thought frantically. What did that mean? Was she happy or sad?

Naturally, he gathered her into his arms—*naturally*—holding her against him till the weeping subsided to the occasional hiccup. By which time Jack was frozen to death standing out there in the wind.

'I think we should go inside,' he said and steered

her back into the living room, shutting the door behind them.

'I'm sorry,' he said unhappily. 'I shouldn't have said
anything. I told myself to be patient but I'm not a patient
man. Now I guess I've ruined everything.'

'No no,' she denied hurriedly, her green eyes glis-
tening as she stared up at him. 'You haven't ruined
anything.'

'I haven't?'

'Jack, I've been in love with you for ages.'

'You have?'

'Yes. I didn't want to say anything either, because I
was hoping you might fall in love with me in the end.
And, yes, of course I'll marry you, my wonderful, marvellous, adorable, darling Jack.' And she reached up to
lay two warm hands against his still-cold cheeks.

It was weird, Jack thought, that happiness could
make a grown man cry. He struggled to blink away
the moisture which suddenly pooled in his eyes. But
it was no use. This was one battle he would not win.

And then it was *her* hugging *him*, telling him over
and over how much she loved him. They cried together,
then kissed, then laughed at each other, calling each
other silly fools for not being honest. After that, they
went downstairs and opened the champagne to celebrate their happiness before heading back upstairs to
cement their love the way couples had been cementing
their love since time began.

The curry wasn't eaten till later that night. Much,
much later.

CHAPTER TWENTY-THREE

IT WAS EARLY summer, three weeks before Christmas. The sky was clear and blue, the air warm and the bride very beautiful.

Not that his Vivienne was ever anything short of beautiful, Jack thought as he held both her hands and looked deep into her lovely green eyes.

They were standing on the same balcony where it had begun all those months ago. The marriage celebrant stood with his back to the view whilst the guests gathered on each side of the bride and groom to witness the ceremony. Not that there were all that many guests. Aside from Jack's mother and George, there was only Marion and her new English husband, Will, along with Jack's two sisters, husbands and children. Of course, Jack's family already adored Vivienne. But who could not? She was a genuinely lovely person.

Jack had bought her an engagement ring the very next day after his proposal, a large baguette diamond with emeralds on the shoulders to match her eyes. But they'd waited till Francesco's Folly's refurbishment was actually complete to get married.

Painted white now, with a new terracotta roof, it sat on top of its hill, standing out like a sparkling jewel, surrounded by the lush green of the surrounding bushland. Inside, the rest of the house was totally transformed. Vivienne had given full rein to her design skills, not making any silly compromises just because she would be living there permanently now. It seemed that telling him about her mother's hoarding had somehow freed her of the anxiety which she associated with clutter, though she still wasn't fond of rooms being over-furnished or overdone. Less was sometimes more, she'd told Jack.

As for colour schemes, she obviously preferred neutral colours, with just splashes of accent colours. She had let her head go a bit with the two apartments downstairs, despite still sticking to her base of white walls, white kitchens and white bathrooms. But there was a lot more colour.

Because children would be occupying the rooms, she'd selected leather lounges and chairs as they were more easy care. And nothing pale: reds and blacks. She'd also used black granite on the various counter tops instead of the brown marble that she'd used upstairs. Again, saying she was thinking of the children, she'd had several bookcases built in to the living rooms to accommodate toys, knick-knacks, photographs and, yes, the odd book or two. Not that children read that much anymore, Jack realised. It was all games consoles and tablets. Jack had been pleased when Vivienne had bought herself a bookcase recently to go in the living room upstairs, a lovely old antique one which was now overflowing with thrillers, none of which Jack had read. Though he kept meaning to.

Vivienne had never returned to live in Sydney, selling her Sydney apartment to Marion and Will. For a bargain price, Jack thought. Not that he cared. He had plenty of money. They'd decided that once the house was finished Jack would divide his time equally between here and Sydney until he could wind up his business down there and start another building company up in the Newcastle area. Vivienne had already set up her own website for a boutique design business, and was receiving quite a few offers of work. She hadn't wanted to try for a baby until they were married—and Jack aimed to get onto that project asap. He was really looking forward to becoming a dad—more than he would have thought possible.

Vivienne giving his fingers a squeeze brought him back to the moment at hand.

'We're now man and wife,' she said with a soft, sweet smile. 'You can kiss me if you like.'

He kissed her while everyone clapped.

'So where were you when the ceremony was taking place?' she whispered after his lips lifted enough for her to speak.

'I was thinking about making you a mother tonight.'

'It doesn't always happen as quickly as that, Jack. We might have to wait months.'

Vivienne was right. She didn't become a mother that night. Though she did fall pregnant early in the New Year. With a boy.

As for Francesco's Folly, it was always a happy home, full of laughter and love. Eventually, Jack and Vivienne had four children: two boys and two girls. Vivienne continued to work, though only part-time. And Jack? He gave up being a workaholic and devoted a lot more time to his family. His mother never married George. But they were still happy, living next to each other and going on endless holidays together. Jack's two sisters and their families often came to stay, especially at Christmas, when all the cousins would have a great time together, having barbeques and going to the beach. In fact, lots of people came to stay with them at Francesco's Folly.

Marion and Will. Even Nigel and his wife. It was that kind of house.

Sometimes, on a balmy summer evening, when Vivienne sat on her favourite balcony sipping a deliciously chilled white wine and drinking in the glorious view, she imagined Francesco up in heaven looking down at her and feeling very content that his lovely home was being lived in and loved. And it was in those moments that she would thank God for saving her from disaster all those years ago and sending her a man like Jack to love.

Her life was not perfect. Whose life was? But it was very good. Very good indeed.

* * * * *

Mills & Boon® Hardback
January 2014

ROMANCE

The Dimitrakos Proposition	Lynne Graham
His Temporary Mistress	Cathy Williams
A Man Without Mercy	Miranda Lee
The Flaw in His Diamond	Susan Stephens
Forged in the Desert Heat	Maisey Yates
The Tycoon's Delicious Distraction	Maggie Cox
A Deal with Benefits	Susanna Carr
The Most Expensive Lie of All	Michelle Conder
The Dance Off	Ally Blake
Confessions of a Bad Bridesmaid	Jennifer Rae
The Greek's Tiny Miracle	Rebecca Winters
The Man Behind the Mask	Barbara Wallace
English Girl in New York	Scarlet Wilson
The Final Falcon Says I Do	Lucy Gordon
Mr (Not Quite) Perfect	Jessica Hart
After the Party	Jackie Braun
Her Hard to Resist Husband	Tina Beckett
Mr Right All Along	Jennifer Taylor

MEDICAL

The Rebel Doc Who Stole Her Heart	Susan Carlisle
From Duty to Daddy	Sue MacKay
Changed by His Son's Smile	Robin Gianna
Her Miracle Twins	Margaret Barker

213 GEN STD HB

Mills & Boon® Large Print
January 2014

ROMANCE

Challenging Dante	Lynne Graham
Captivated by Her Innocence	Kim Lawrence
Lost to the Desert Warrior	Sarah Morgan
His Unexpected Legacy	Chantelle Shaw
Never Say No to a Caffarelli	Melanie Milburne
His Ring Is Not Enough	Maisey Yates
A Reputation to Uphold	Victoria Parker
Bound by a Baby	Kate Hardy
In the Line of Duty	Ami Weaver
Patchwork Family in the Outback	Soraya Lane
The Rebound Guy	Fiona Harper

HISTORICAL

Mistress at Midnight	Sophia James
The Runaway Countess	Amanda McCabe
In the Commodore's Hands	Mary Nichols
Promised to the Crusader	Anne Herries
Beauty and the Baron	Deborah Hale

MEDICAL

Dr Dark and Far-Too Delicious	Carol Marinelli
Secrets of a Career Girl	Carol Marinelli
The Gift of a Child	Sue MacKay
How to Resist a Heartbreaker	Louisa George
A Date with the Ice Princess	Kate Hardy
The Rebel Who Loved Her	Jennifer Taylor

Mills & Boon® Hardback
February 2014

ROMANCE

A Bargain with the Enemy	Carole Mortimer
A Secret Until Now	Kim Lawrence
Shamed in the Sands	Sharon Kendrick
Seduction Never Lies	Sara Craven
When Falcone's World Stops Turning	Abby Green
Securing the Greek's Legacy	Julia James
An Exquisite Challenge	Jennifer Hayward
A Debt Paid in Passion	Dani Collins
The Last Guy She Should Call	Joss Wood
No Time Like Mardi Gras	Kimberly Lang
Daring to Trust the Boss	Susan Meier
Rescued by the Millionaire	Cara Colter
Heiress on the Run	Sophie Pembroke
The Summer They Never Forgot	Kandy Shepherd
Trouble On Her Doorstep	Nina Harrington
Romance For Cynics	Nicola Marsh
Melting the Ice Queen's Heart	Amy Ruttan
Resisting Her Ex's Touch	Amber McKenzie

MEDICAL

Tempted by Dr Morales	Carol Marinelli
The Accidental Romeo	Carol Marinelli
The Honourable Army Doc	Emily Forbes
A Doctor to Remember	Joanna Neil

Mills & Boon® Large Print
February 2014

ROMANCE

The Greek's Marriage Bargain	Sharon Kendrick
An Enticing Debt to Pay	Annie West
The Playboy of Puerto Banús	Carol Marinelli
Marriage Made of Secrets	Maya Blake
Never Underestimate a Caffarelli	Melanie Milburne
The Divorce Party	Jennifer Hayward
A Hint of Scandal	Tara Pammi
Single Dad's Christmas Miracle	Susan Meier
Snowbound with the Soldier	Jennifer Faye
The Redemption of Rico D'Angelo	Michelle Douglas
Blame It on the Champagne	Nina Harrington

HISTORICAL

A Date with Dishonour	Mary Brendan
The Master of Stonegrave Hall	Helen Dickson
Engagement of Convenience	Georgie Lee
Defiant in the Viking's Bed	Joanna Fulford
The Adventurer's Bride	June Francis

MEDICAL

Miracle on Kaimotu Island	Marion Lennox
Always the Hero	Alison Roberts
The Maverick Doctor and Miss Prim	Scarlet Wilson
About That Night...	Scarlet Wilson
Daring to Date Dr Celebrity	Emily Forbes
Resisting the New Doc In Town	Lucy Clark